Took You So Long

C . I . M A T T H E W S

The Porcupine's Quill

Library and Archives Canada Cataloguing in Publication

Title: Took you so long / C.I. Matthews.
Names: Matthews, C.I., author.
Description: Short stories.
Identifiers: Canadiana (print) 20220394903 | Canadiana (ebook) 20220394911
    | ISBN 9780889844469 (softcover) | ISBN 9780889844476 (PDF)
Subjects: LCGFT: Short stories.
Classification: LCC PS8626.A858 T66 2022 | DDC C813/.6—dc23

Published by The Porcupine's Quill, 68 Main Street, PO Box 160,
Erin, Ontario NOB 1T0. http://porcupinesquill.ca

Edited by Stephanie Small. Represented in Canada by Canadian Manda.
Trade orders are available from University of Toronto Press.

We acknowledge the support of the Ontario Arts Council and the Canada
Council for the Arts for our publishing program. The financial support of the
Government of Canada is also gratefully acknowledged.

Canada Council   Conseil des arts
for the Arts   du Canada

ONTARIO ARTS COUNCIL
CONSEIL DES ARTS DE L'ONTARIO
an Ontario government agency
un organisme du gouvernement de l'Ontario

Canadä

Ontario
Ontario Media Development
Corporation

In memory of my parents—

Otto Alois König (1929–1992)
Theresia König (1929–2006)

TABLE OF CONTENTS

THE HOLE

Kathryn Maxwell tumbled into a hole right after lunch. It wasn't much of a lunch, just reheated sausage, a slice of day-old bread, and half a can of beer left over from the night before. A good enough feed to put a kick in her step. All morning, she'd had her sights set on sinking her teeth into something better than leftovers, something shamelessly succulent.

For weeks she'd been obsessing about getting her hands on morels. The fungi predictably sprang forth after the long winter, under a grove of burr oaks in the far corner of her ten-acre property. The spot was shady and moist with loamy soil, ideal conditions for morels. Kathryn hated paying good money at the farmers' market for something she could get in her own fields for free, and besides, hers were much fresher.

If she picked the morels when they were small and young, there was nothing like them. Sautéed in butter and crushed garlic, the nutty, meaty flavour titillated the taste buds. The distinctive honeycomb ridges, a French tickler of pits and caps, offered sensual delight. True, a morel was a pain to clean, with its hollow exterior of irregular bumpy holes and ridges, but *Morchella*, with its unique anatomical perfection, guaranteed a gustatory climax without the mess and aggravation of sex.

On this particular Saturday in May, instead of picking morels, Kathryn was breast deep in a sinkhole—straight, long, and, for all Kathryn knew, bottomless. One thing for sure, her feet were not touching ground. Luckily, her wide hips were wedged against a rock; otherwise, her whole body might have fallen in. As it was, her head and shoulders were sticking out of the hole and her arms were splayed out on either side.

It was no wonder she'd missed seeing the hole. It was shrouded by ferns whose leaves were enormous, at least from her ground-level point of view. She reached for several stalks hoping to gain some leverage to pull herself out, but the ferns, too delicate to bear her weight, uprooted when she pulled on them.

She reached for the basket she'd been holding when she fell in. It had landed on its side against a rock. Straining and stretching her left arm as far as it would go, she managed to grasp the wooden handle and drag the basket towards her. She wedged it across the narrow space between her breasts and the edge of the hole, but the basket was made for carrying morels, and it broke when she put her weight on it.

From her vantage point, Kathryn could see this wasn't the only hole on the property. The place was riddled with them. Not that the hole she was in had been made by gophers necessarily, but she'd been after Norman, her neighbour and occasional lover, to shoot whatever the hell had turned the property into a holey mess. Norman told her he was reluctant to raise a .22 at them, as his eyesight wasn't what it used to be.

When she was younger and had the wherewithal to bother with a creature-sensitive pest-management strategy, Kathryn and her then-husband, Stan, had gone to the trouble of setting live traps. But that was then, when she had been a perkier version of herself, working as a human resources manager at the credit union, a person who took charge—of rodents and unmotivated people alike. A person who assessed workplace incompetence, determined solutions, and set traps to catch staff not pulling their weight. Now she was the one who was trapped.

Stan had hated gophers as much as she did. When the live traps turned out to be a useless solution, he had tied gasoline-soaked rags to the end of a pole. Once he was sure the animal was underground, he lit the end of the pole and smoked the bastards to death. After, he filled the holes in with rocks and soil so no other gophers could adopt the tunnels made by their erstwhile brethren.

When she'd told Norman the story about Stan's rodent-ridding technique, he had laughed. 'They've got canisters at the Co-op that do that now. Save your money. They don't work.'

But Norman still had a trick up his sleeve.

'Pneumonia. They can't stand pneumonia,' he had said, combing his fingers through his thin grey hair.

'Surely you mean ammonia,' Kathryn had replied.

'Right. That's what they don't like.'

Ammonia. How awful. She could barely stand the idea of suffocating them but they *had* taken over. In the end, since she didn't want to risk Norman feeling like an incompetent fool if he failed to shoot the pests, she told him to go ahead and use the ammonia.

Kathryn knew all about not feeling reliable or competent. When she had been employed in human resources, she knew staff griped about her, that they felt trapped by her autocratic management style. Their voices had gone silent whenever she entered the staff lounge. It seemed fitting that in her retirement the universe had decided to turn her into a prisoner.

She tried to relax her body. Her toes, feet, legs, all the way up. Even her arms and eyes. It was most challenging to calm her eyes. The wind had picked up, ground-level grit spraying directly into her eyes and mouth. Wiping them did little to relieve the burning irritation.

If only she had access to Stan's eye drops, something he used to keep his eyes lubricated and make them less itchy. But he'd packed up the drops and every other item he owned when he decided to end the marriage. If only she'd recognized the signs that their relationship had been crumbling. She had often stayed late in the office, and she never considered rushing home to spend the evenings with him. So, he'd begun to make his own fun. Said he'd joined a cribbage group that met a couple of evenings a week. Mondays and Wednesdays were reserved for darts. At first, he'd leave a small supper plate for her in the fridge but eventually that stopped, too.

Once she had begun to suspect that the marriage might be destined for the toilet, her heart and lungs had felt as if they no longer fit inside her chest. She believed she still loved Stan. Sure, she had a hard time showing it. Prior to their break up, they hadn't had sexual relations in months, or maybe even years.

One night a few years back, after a particularly uncomfortable performance appraisal meeting with a union-savvy staff member, Kathryn had arrived home to find the house empty. Eventually, she discovered that darts and cribbage were lies. That a woman named Anaïs had been sucking Stan's dick. That the Parisian-born husband-stealer had whispered *oui oui* instead of *non non* when Stan lured her into an empty classroom instead of supervising the school dance — or had she lured him?

If Kathryn had been more present in the marriage, had sustained an ongoing, passionate interest in Stan, had not permitted work to overtake her every waking moment, perhaps his love for her would not have chilled.

During morel season, the temperature could be cool and crisp one moment and sultry the next. At this particular moment it was ticklish-warm and sticky. The wind carrying the grit no longer plagued her. In fact, there was no longer any breeze to speak of, and Kathryn found herself now bothered by black flies. Thank God her hands were free so she could slap her neck and face before they could bite. However, each time she made a sudden jarring movement of her upper body, a searing pain shot down her leg.

Perspiration beaded her forehead and upper lip. She could

taste salt and realized she was very, very thirsty. How long had she been stuck? When was the last time she'd had a drink of water? Would that bird circling overhead decide she looked good enough to eat and start picking at her? What if she couldn't manage to pull herself out by nightfall? Were the walls of the hole actually crushing her chest or was this nothing more than a panic attack? What was that gummy thing caught in her throat? It felt large, as if it could smother her. How long would she be able to survive out here? Was she going crazy?

Despite Stan insisting they attend church every Sunday, Kathryn wasn't the praying kind. She wasn't the sort to buy into the idea of religion as a path toward goodness. But at times like this, she wished Stan were here to encourage her by whispering in her ear that she could pray without feeling like a fraud. She wished she could believe that the act of prayer would have any tangible effort on her situation. But really, what was the use?

She tried to free herself once more, pressing her elbows and forearms against the ground and trying to push herself up. 'Damn it!' she yelled, cursing herself for not having stuck with the exercise program her family doctor suggested she start in January. But, like so many who make resolutions, she'd stopped cycling on her stationary bike by week three. With no Stan to lose weight for, there had been no point in continuing. She remained stuck at forty pounds over her ideal weight.

It occurred to Kathryn that her leg might be broken. She could feel it swelling beneath her. She tried not to dwell on the throbbing but, because she'd never broken a bone before, she couldn't be certain if this was what a broken leg was supposed to feel like. All she knew was she could feel her heart beating in her toes.

Suddenly Kathryn heard the clatter of metal. Norman, tilling the field next to hers. He'd mentioned only last week after an afternoon quickie that he intended to grow pulses, some kind of soya or something. She'd stopped paying attention when the conversation got technical. Now she'd give anything to hear his technical babble if only he'd look her way right at this moment.

She frantically waved her arms in hopes of attracting his attention. 'Help!' she yelled. 'Help!' She could see Norman so clearly through breaks in the ferns, but the tractor he was riding drowned out her voice. Quick as a gopher running for cover, Norman and the tractor vanished over a hill.

Kathryn had never been one to join clubs. Stan used to say he found some of her attributes strange but endearing. How she didn't watch TV. How she drank Pepsi first thing in the morning, never a hot beverage. How she didn't stand for gossip. How she didn't attend organized events like community suppers or union meetings. As a child, she'd resisted her mother's urgings to sign up for Brownies or Girl Guides. If only she had complied, maybe now she'd know how to pull herself out of this absurd, ridiculous, impossible situation.

'Stan always said I was a square peg in a round hole!' She giggled. And then she started to laugh hysterically at her own stupid joke. 'Calm down,' she told herself sternly.

Kathryn tried to visualize the moments prior to falling into the hole. She thought if she could rewind the video in her mind, she might be able to see a way out.

She inhaled the silence of the afternoon, breathed in the musty scent of the soil. She closed her eyes and permitted fatigue to wash over her. As if in a dream, she saw herself plucking through the field, the trefoil, plantain, and vetches ankle-deep, heading for the ferny patch at the edge of the woods. If only she'd worn proper shoes, she thought. Runners or Merrell hikers. Sturdy footwear to prevent her from falling, keep her steady and upright. But, no, she lived in her Birkenstocks, one of which she could feel had already slipped off.

She kicked off the other and waited to hear the thump or

splash as it hit the bottom. She counted the seconds—one one thousand, two one thousand, three one thousand—but heard nothing.

Walking through the gloriously green patch of ferns, the basket clutched to her chest, her attention had been rooted on the morels, on the buttery taste and complex honeycomb texture against her tongue. And then it was as if she were a character in a fairy tale, as if she'd suddenly been swallowed by a whale or been pushed by a bully into an abandoned well.

A jolt of pain shot through her gut. One of those pesky digestive cramps again. She could see the medication to stop loose bowels on her bathroom counter. What could she do if diarrhea just started running down her leg? No wonder Stan had followed his sexual urges and allowed Anaïs to seduce him. Kathryn was nothing but a lousy, broken specimen. She wouldn't love her either, if she were Stan.

Kathryn shouted, 'I'm going fucking insane here!'

Summoning her last ounce of strength, Kathryn's hands scrabbled in the dirt, her fingers, twisted with arthritis, weak and ineffective. Her eyes welled up.

And then she remembered: she'd had a sudden wave of vertigo right before falling. It had hit her hard, like a car door opening into the path of an unsuspecting cyclist. The ground had started spinning, like it did when she and Stan rode the Tilt-A-Whirl at the fall fair. Her balance felt distorted, as if she were on rollerblades for the first time. She had stumbled toward the morels with all the grace of a drunkard. And there had been that insistent ringing in her ears, like a bug had flown into her Eustachian tube, its wings madly flapping to free itself.

When a kettle of turkey vultures hovered overhead, Kathryn froze. It hurt to raise her head up to watch them dip and soar. She could feel the start of a headache brewing right above her eyebrows. What if one of the birds swooped down and began plucking out her eyes? It occurred to Kathryn that she might never see her pottery again, what she fondly called her functional art collection, presents Stan had purchased for special occasions such as birthdays and Christmas. Her hutch was filled with hand-made bowls, platters, tiny pickle dishes. Try as she might, she couldn't remember the last time she and Stan had entertained with those items.

She and Stan. Gosh, how she ached for him. The stroke of his pinkie against her cheek. How he'd bring her a Pepsi every Saturday morning. The trips to the farmers' market for garlic scapes, fresh tomatoes, and herbs they couldn't successfully grow. Sitting on the porch next to each other, sharing sections of the newspaper. Laughing over the cartoons together. She never would have guessed in a hundred decades that she'd have to face retirement alone.

Off in the distance, where Norman had been plowing the field, was a lake, wet and blue and wobbly. Only it wasn't a lake, it was a mirage. God, Kathryn was thirsty. If she could get there by crawling, she'd lap at the water like a dog. She wished she were the sort to keep a water bottle on hand.

It was then, for the first time, that true panic washed over her. Again, desperately, she pushed against the soil, but to no avail. When had she gotten so weak? She could hear Stan's voice worming into her ear, 'You've always been weak!' Much as she missed him, she still remembered how mean he could be.

'Somebody pl-ea-se help me!' she called.

She closed her eyes so she could breathe through the throbbing in her leg.

She wiped her forehead with the gnarled fingers of her right hand and vowed, if she survived the hole, she would try to better understand the reasons why Stan had dumped her. And consider making changes. Maybe even see a counsellor, like Stan had suggested more than once in their time together.

Stan had been a looker in his day. Strong, broad-chested, with heavily muscled arms and a thin gap between his top teeth, the whitest teeth she'd ever seen. And his smile—it left her randy with longing. But he had been a wanderer right from the beginning. Anaïs wasn't the first and wouldn't be the last. She had to keep that in mind if she ever seriously thought of reconciling with Stan.

Suddenly, in front of her, was a man. Had Stan known to look for her, and if so, how? Or, was it another mirage? His head was backlit by the late afternoon sun, his shoulders as big as mountains, his thighs twin oaks of strength.

'Help me,' Kathryn managed to utter.

Her head sank against her chest. Her eyes closed. Where was the man now? She waited to feel his huge hands lifting her up, pulling her to safety. She squeezed her fingers into the dirt and, just before she lost consciousness, promised to find a way back to Stan.

LOVINA

Good thing I clipped that ad about the new clinic before Eli tossed the *Penny Saver* into the burn barrel. We're expecting again. Eli isn't sure about having a midwife this time, on account of me losing the first baby, a boy we called Timothy after my grandfather. The clinic doesn't open until eleven. What a waste of a day. People around here should know that the farming community is early to bed and early to rise. If only Eli hadn't rushed me around this morning, I wouldn't have forgotten my list of questions on the kitchen counter.

I look a mess. I wish I'd known my dress and apron were crooked. I had everything pinned properly before we left the house. Grandmother Miriam used to say that an Amish woman ought to be able to pin her apron straight even if she's in a coffin.

I can't believe how often I have to pee. I can't stand public toilets. My sisters and I were taught to nudge the stall door open with our shoulders and use our foot on the flusher. I hate people who don't flush. Not an issue at home because we use an outhouse.

Thank goodness I brought the ad, otherwise I'd never remember the address. We don't often find ourselves on Chandler Street. The plan was to do a bit of shopping then grab something at McDonald's before heading to the appointment. Eli loves their fries but I find them salty. If I dilly-dally around here much longer, Eli will lose it. Oh, to heck with the clinic; I don't feel like going anymore.

My feet are achy, especially the ankles. I'll soak them later in a footbath of stale bread and warm milk. It's our community's preferred choice over fancy, store-bought remedies. It'll do wonders for my temper. Maybe it's my blood sugar. I only had a cup of St. John's wort that Eli brewed for me. When I make it, it's too strong. He says it's because I let the water boil on and on. I should have eaten, but my stomach has been up and down again.

Look at that Eli, so handsome with his arms crossed, pressed against the window of McDonald's.

'You didn't buy anything, Lovina.'

Deep inside my dress pocket there's a metal toy soldier and a drink umbrella. I lifted them from Dollarama. If he finds out, I'll be in for it.

I force myself to smile. 'Nothing caught my interest. You know how fussy I can be.' Once inside, I say, 'I could eat three Big Macs. Do you mind?'

Eli rests a hand on my belly. 'My lovely Mrs Kuepfer, nothing would please me more.'

I twist away. 'Stop it. You'll make people gawk.'

* * *

Eli adjusts the bit in Belle's mouth before finger-measuring the throat latch. He climbs into the buggy and thinks, *Not another of Lovina's moods.* She's got herself squished against the other side of the buggy as if terrified Eli will give her fleas. He can't stand these episodes. She caught on to this way of acting from her mother, a woman with a jittery temperament who was prone to long bouts of crying. Sure, he expected Lovina to feel blue after they lost Timothy. It was rough on him, too. He prayed hard and got on with things until God thankfully graced them with this new baby.

It wasn't always this way. When they were courting, she smiled and teased him during softball games after Sunday service.

She used to enjoy the clip-clop of Belle's hooves and the sway of the buggy. The simple life satisfied her. Now, he gingerly steps around her.

Once home, he stows the buggy before pasturing Belle. He leaves Lovina to wait for him under the quaking aspen, the hoeing postponed until after the footbath. After giving Belle a treat of apples, he pulls out his handkerchief and mops Lovina's brow. 'You deserve a rest,' he tells her. 'Next week we'll try the clinic again.'

She rolls her eyes.

After Eli fetches a basin with the foot soak remedy, he sprawls on the ground next to Lovina and studies his wife of two years. Since Timothy died, life had been a trial. Lovina's problems weren't something you could discuss with just anyone. Everyone has troubles, and he and Lovina are responsible for their own. Is it because she was only eighteen, barely a child, when they married? He wonders if other young wives experience such darkness.

He peers over her shoulder down the treed lane, trying to imagine what the future holds.

'Cat got your tongue?' he says, his hand at his brow blocking the sun.

What Lovina has is akin to a virus that comes and goes. Some days she's a typical Amish woman with her eye on family, the kitchen and garden, and the matrimonial bed. Other times, it's as if a thick chunk of firewood destined for the cookstove beats down her very essence. At those times, it's like she's up and gone missing.

'The foot soak helping?' He removes his going-to-town hat and finger-combs his bangs.

She whacks his face. 'Eli, above your lip, there's a woolly bear. You know what that means? A bad omen.'

Eli clutches her wrist. 'You're having another episode.'

She answers by heading for the house, her wet footprints

leaving a trail behind her in the grass. 'The hoeing will wait.' She waves a dismissive hand.

He shakes his head. Four o'clock. Another night he'll be scrounging for supper.

* * *

I go up to bed after my foot soak. It's not even suppertime but I'm completely wrung out. Then I start crying and can't stop. I go from crying to laughing and back to crying. It's all Eli's fault. He kept going on and on about nothing. Sometimes even to hear his voice is enough to make a woman crazy.

The Amish follow the scriptures as they were written, but there are times our people can be mean. When our community meets up at the market or at auction, we like to whisper about the weakest members of the flock. Take Rebecca. In love with Samuel until for some reason they broke things off. Then she went completely nutty. Started slicing up her sheets and blankets. Another time she stripped off her clothes and pranced around naked in public. Her parents couldn't make her stop so they locked her in the shed behind the house. Somebody tried to sneak her out but her father chased them off. Rebecca slipped away one night and no one has seen her since. The worst is if she returns, she won't be allowed to stay. Her family would send her off again, not wanting her shame to taint them further.

Soft constitution. That is what people call it. Too delicate. Some people keep everything inside and then, kaboom. I'm not saying that's what's going on with me. I'm just saying that's how it is with some of our community, those with thinking problems.

* * *

Lovina's contractions coincide with the full moon. They are strong and persistent, like they mean business.

'It's too early,' Lovina tells Eli. 'Not again. Please, not again.'

Eli paces the hallway, wringing his hands. If only they had a telephone. But their community follows the *Ordnung* and doesn't subscribe to modern technologies. If they did, he'd be able to call the midwife straight away.

Eli can't stand to see Lovina like this, her knees bent, toes curled like talons, lips pursed. Her shrieks of pain echo through the house. The smell of iron filings fills the air. There is so much blood. Lovina's having serious woman trouble, but what's Eli to do? It's too soon. *This* isn't supposed to happen until November. Eli shouldn't leave Lovina in the throes of labour, yet he knows he has no choice; he must fetch the midwife.

'I'll manage,' Lovina says before shuddering with another contraction. Her face is the colour of ash.

Eli hitches up Belle. By the time he returns with the midwife, the infant is on Lovina's chest, the cord tight around the baby's neck.

'No, it can't be,' Eli says, squeezing his thighs with his hands.

The midwife whisks the child away.

Before long Lovina heals—physically. She is, after all, a sturdy Amish wife.

Late one night, weeks after laying their second son to rest, Eli awakens to a rasping noise. His socked feet descend the steps to the cellar where he finds Lovina sitting on a low wooden stool, magazines scattered on the floor. He sighs before saying, 'Lovina, what are you doing? Come to bed.'

She's so focused on the task at hand that she leaps at the sound of his voice. She looks at him with red-rimmed eyes. 'What does it look like I'm doing? I'm papering.'

A small ceramic bowl containing a mixture of flour and water sits to her left, a paintbrush on the floor beside it. Cutouts from magazines of women's faces, garish with neon lips, painted eyelids, and oversized glasses, look down from the opposite wall. On the floor by her feet are pictures of babies, all sizes and colours.

'Your work is done here.'

'Don't you dare tell me what to do,' she says.

He rests a hand on her shoulder. She whips around and squirts out of reach, wielding the scissors. She stabs the air between them.

'Lovina, I'm warning you.'

'Why, what are you going to do?'

She's worse than he's ever seen her. He's faced with a tough decision: run for the horsewhip or leave her be.

As he mounts the stairs to the shed, Lovina sneers. 'Coward!'

* * *

My name is Sarah Elizabeth Yoder, but I go by Susie. I'm the hired girl that poor Mr Kuepfer took in to help out around the house. I probably shouldn't say this but honestly, his wife is a piece of work. Don't think less of me, but I've been writing everything, and I mean everything, in a hardcover book I picked up at a yard sale. Wrote last night that Mr Kuepfer works day and night to give his wife a good life, and you know how she pays him back? She's been wetting the bed. Too ignorant, I tell you, to get her arse to the outhouse. If she thinks I'm going to change diapers, she's got another think coming.

* * *

Eli does what any good husband would do. Offers Lovina licorice root tonic. Prays. Massages her heels and Achilles tendons. Gives her B12 and folic acid, supplements the naturopath recommended. Sings hymns. Reads from the scriptures. Considers getting her hair tested for metal poisoning. Applies menthol to her temples. And what thanks does he get? She accuses him of bedding down with Susie.

* * *

You won't believe Mrs Kuepfer now, her groaning and carrying on.

'Susie, bring the bedpan,' Lovina says, moaning.

Do I look like a nurse? I've decided to share my journal with Mr Kuepfer. See if that fixes Mrs Lazybones once and for all. People are talking. Saying poor Mr Kuepfer this and poor Mr Kuepfer that. I never signed up for this. I'm leaving. The Lapps need someone to watch the twins while the Missus tends to the garden. Even if Mr Kuepfer doubled my salary, it's not worth it. My mother says what Mrs Kuepfer needs most is a swift kick up the backside.

* * *

Eli records his observations in a scribbler tucked inside his book-keeping register. The strain of being responsible for the business, farm, Lovina, and her duties leaves dark smudges under his usually bright eyes.

When he drops by his mother-in-law's, she asks, 'How long has it been going on?'

'Forever.'

'She's begging for help, Eli. Don't miss the opportunity. I had my share of dark days, you might recall.'

'I've been doing so much for her but none of it helps.'

'It's your duty.'

'I don't know how much longer—'

'What are you saying?' she asks, her eyes somber behind thick lenses.

'Can she stay here? Just a couple of nights?'

'I've done my part,' she says. 'Go be with her, read to her from the scriptures.' She goes to a drawer and removes a cellphone. 'You need this more than I do.'

His initial impulse is to refuse the technology as cellphones are frowned upon by the community, but he pockets it anyway.

'Go home. Be the good man my daughter married.'

Back in the buggy, he lifts his face to meet the unrelenting fall wind. When he approaches his laneway, he considers going past the farm and leaving Lovina to fend for herself. But, if he did, the community would most certainly shun him.

For the last while, Eli has been sleeping on the horsehair sofa. Every night right before retiring, he checks on Lovina. On this particular night he notices a foul smell. He pushes the door in to find Lovina slumped on the floor, an empty pill bottle next to her. He chucks it at the wall before fumbling for the cellphone. A wave of shame washes over him when he is forced to reveal to the operator that his wife has tried to take her life.

* * *

Eli is excused from Sunday worship. A neighbour drives him to Philhaven, the psychiatric facility in the next borough.

There's a long wooden bench in the foyer. This is where children wait while their parents visit loved ones. Most Sundays the same little girl sits on the bench. There's paper, a toy train and a small box next to her. From her pocket she pulls a round of summer sausage. A man in a blue uniform stands guard at the entrance to the long-stay unit.

'Hello,' Eli says to the girl. 'Nice to see you again.'

She opens her mouth to speak, then thinks better of it. She offers him some sausage.

'Who are you waiting for today?' he asks.

She answers by tipping the box over. Two crayons clatter onto the linoleum.

He points at the floor. 'Where are the rest?'

'Mommy ate them.'

* * *

People in the community give Eli the impression he is a man who hasn't managed his wife well. The bishop has told Eli they should try for another baby after Lovina's release. By now Eli should be wearing a flat crowned hat, the kind worn by Amish fathers. If only he lived closer to his parents. They'd know what he should do. What had the bishop said? That some of the flock will stray, and that when that happens, the community adjusts to their absence. The bishop called Lovina's condition *a debilitating illness of faith*.

* * *

I'm waiting for Eli in the common room. It's where patients receive visitors. I'm so nervous. Eli should be here by now. The doctor finally added him back onto the visitor roster. I got in trouble in group therapy when I said my illness comes from God. Dr Bradshaw explained that I was scaring the other patients, especially those who don't believe. Now I have to take a blue pill, a pink one, and two white ones. I wish I didn't. They leave me feeling groggy.

Dr Bradshaw doesn't get how my illness makes me stronger. That I'm thinking all the time, even when I'm supposed to be sleeping. I wish I could stop rocking. Eli said I'm wasting away. Dr Bradshaw told me to be patient, to give the medicine time to work. Last week Mary Jane spit her tablets into the water fountain. Dr Bradshaw says we should never do this. The orderlies and nurses have been watching us. We have to show our tongues and the inside of our mouths at medication time now, right after swallowing.

The people playing cribbage by the door are too noisy. They're not supposed to yell out when they get a good hand. Eli hates loud noises. If it's noisy, he might not want to come in.

I made Eli a coffee. If he doesn't come soon, it'll be cold. The coffee here tastes burnt. My mouth is dry as lint. Dr Bradshaw says Eli saved my life, and that it's time for me to face that I have a mental illness. The Amish don't use those words. My mother suffered something like this, too. Dr Bradshaw calls it bipolar disorder. That means I get really sad or super angry mixed with happy. The pills mess up my memory. Yesterday I couldn't remember if I was allowed to take a dinner roll, and if I was, which kind, whole wheat or white, so I took both. Then the cook yelled at me for not leaving enough for others. I wanted to punch her.

The patients drag their feet along the floor like three-toed sloths. I read about sloths in a magazine with a yellow cover. I'd better remember to ask Eli to bring me new house shoes. Mine are falling apart.

He's late. I know because I've checked the clock a million times. Dr Bradshaw tells me to pay attention to clues that my anxiety is going up. Then I'm supposed to do four-square breathing. I find it helpful. I breathe in for four breaths, hold for two, exhale for four, and hold for two. It can be quite calming. Some of the other patients can hold their inhale and exhale for a count of eight. I could never do that.

The chair where Eli is supposed to sit looks crooked. Every time I move it, it makes a sound like a dog scratching its ear.

I'd better make Eli another cup of coffee. The other one is cold.

* * *

'Hello Lovina.'

'Eli, you startled me,' I say, stirring his coffee with my fingertip. 'Here, drink.'

'Thanks.' He sets the summer sausage on the table next to my hand. I'm not hungry but I take a bite so Eli will think I like that he brought something nice. There's too much garlic for my taste.

'What have you been doing?' His face is blank, like a chalkboard during summer vacation.

Oh, no, I'm supposed to have something nice to share back.

What *have* I been doing? Sweat pools under the purple shirt and trousers they make us wear. I have to be dressed in this, even though Amish women only wear dresses. Eli complained but the administrators say they have no choice. That's what you put up with in a publicly funded hospital.

I wish I could quit rocking. There's spittle in the corner of my lips and I'm having a heck of a time ungluing my tongue from the roof of my mouth. This isn't how the visit is supposed to go.

'The pills make it hard.' I squeeze my eyes closed and try to breathe my worries away.

* * *

Back home, Eli heads into the kitchen, pulls out a chair, and sits a while. He wonders if Lovina will ever be ready to return to him. If the community will ever accept her. Of course, it doesn't help that Susie has been talking. She has told everyone who will listen about Mrs Kuepfer's laziness and Mr Kuepfer's weakness. How it must be their lack of faith that causes God to punish them as He has. Eli worries the entire Amish community will feel as Susie does. But perhaps it is God's will after all.

Eli stands, stretches his arms into the air before heading to the chicken coop to collect eggs for his supper.

GOOSE

As the moving van pulled up to our new townhouse, a girl waved from the front porch of a house across the street. Her long pink hair cascaded down her back. She had a narrow nose and small blue eyes. Hers was the face of a model, the skin free of blemishes, freckles, and stains. Her chest strained against the fabric of her top. When she came toward me, she walked with a limp.

'I'm Rosemarie,' she said, 'but everyone calls me Goose.' When she spoke, she whistled through her teeth.

My looks were the opposite of hers. I didn't even need a training bra yet, and my stomach was so flat it indented. I was the shortest girl in my grade eight class. My hair was buzzed up the sides and back, all the rage with kids my age.

From that point on, Goose and I did everything together, except if she had something on, which was rare. When I was stuck at home, I stood at my bedroom window waiting for her to shuffle across the street toward my house. Despite the limp, Goose liked to walk long distances. Sometimes she didn't look before stepping off the sidewalk, like it never occurred to her to wait for a break in traffic, often causing cars to brake and swerve. She was the sort of person who'd sooner surprise you than not, the sort who might go around with a gun because one happened to be lying around the house. She was reckless that way. She went through life without a care for the harm she might cause herself or others.

Goose did things our classmates never considered. While they wore flared jeans, she wore a dirty lab coat over track pants.

She hitchhiked to the next town to get her nose pierced, later insisting on a full refund when the nostril got infected. She couldn't stand the feel of underwear so she went without.

'Follow me,' she said to me one day after class.

She pushed ahead with confidence while I followed at her heels. We passed kids from school hanging out on their porches, and a few sharing a cigarette in front of the grocery store. One of them hobbled in front of her, making a huge production of dragging his leg,

'Get lost, ya gimp,' Goose said. She didn't seem to react much to their meanness. She never swore, just called kids who made fun of her psychos, or gave them the finger. If I were her, I'd have cared. Reputation is golden to kids our age.

I was tempted to ask what had happened to cause Goose's limp. If she'd been in an accident or been born that way or if a disease had caused it. But since it never naturally came up in conversation, I decided to keep my nosiness to myself.

Goose liked to talk, mostly about the neighbourhood, and as we traipsed all over town, she told me about places that were cool and some that were not.

Once we arrived at the hardware store, she took me by the shoulders and said, 'Give me your word that you won't hang around here.'

'What's the big deal? It's just a hardware store.'

'You have to promise. Never ever go around back by yourself. Especially to the horse hitch.'

I stared back, wide-eyed. 'I wasn't planning to. Besides, why would I want to go to a horse hitch?'

'If you forget and go, I'll know.'

She pulled a folding knife from her pocket. Then she told me to hold out my thumb. Before I knew it, she poked the end of it into my skin. 'Ouch,' I said, pulling my hand away. 'What did you do that for?'

She cut an X into her palm before mixing my blood with hers. 'From now on, all promises are forever.'

I couldn't understand why she didn't want me to hang out there. Was she afraid I'd get kicked or might slip on horse shit? When I asked, she just shrugged.

Goose liked to talk about her parents, how her dad had left when she was two and how her mom now lived with a guy Goose didn't much like.

'We're not compatible.'

I liked that she used words like compatible. Sophisticated sounding words.

'He likes the house at a certain temperature and gets me in trouble when I turn up the thermostat.' She stopped on the sidewalk in front of the used bookstore before saying, 'Sometimes when I bitch too much, my mom lifts her hand and tells me to zip my face or she'll do it for me.'

* * *

One day after early dismissal I headed for Goose's with my backpack of homework. The house was empty except for us. We went up to her bedroom, a room she shared with a much older sister who was away at college. There was nowhere to sit but on the double bed, which was next to a window facing an alley. Across from a chest of drawers were sheets of foolscap thumb-tacked to the wall. Someone had printed with permanent black marker: *You are often the life of the party* and *your smile brightens everyone's day* and *practice makes perfect.*

'What's all this?' I asked, pointing at the messages.

'It's time you minded your own business.' Goose hobbled over to the sheets, ripped them off the wall, and crumpled them up.

We played twenty questions. She went first. Do you like coffee? Best memory? Do you wear underwear? Have you ever been in love? Do skeletons have to eat? Favourite potato: mashed or fries? Have you had your period yet? On and on. Questions I could answer without much thought.

When it was my turn, I asked a few easy ones before posing the zinger.

'Why do you walk with a limp?'

I felt relief to finally have the opportunity to ask until I noticed how serious her face had become. Her eyes were closed as she sat on the edge of the bed, her body swaying back and forth. I stopped breathing.

It was her silence I couldn't stand. I began to imagine what she might say if only she could find her voice: *Shut your face. That's personal. Real friends don't ask about that.*

I didn't push. She'd made it clear she didn't want to talk about it. It wasn't until much later that I discovered she'd had seven surgeries over the course of her childhood and was due for another after her next growth spurt.

* * *

When the school year ended, we spent every moment together. Our mutual affection was electric, the air filled with love.

One Saturday she pulled a fat cigar from her back pocket. 'I borrowed this from my stepdad's stash. It's from his barber who brings them back from Cuba.'

It took three matches to get the cigar going. She passed it to me but I waved it off.

'Pussy!' she said, taking another drag. 'People smoke to calm their nerves.'

'Is that why you do it?'

'No, I'm just saying.'

Across from us were low-income apartments next to what my mom called 'getting-there houses' next to two-storey stone mansions. Not what one expected in a small town. By now we were at the playground next to our school. Goose was on the swing and I sat facing her, my legs straddling her hips.

'Do you shave?' she asked. 'You know, down there?'

'What do you mean?'

'Your crotch? Do you shave it?' she asked.

I didn't want her knowing that I didn't need to.

'Does it hurt?' I asked.

'What? Shaving?'

'My legs around you like this?'

She didn't answer. Instead, she held the cigar to my mouth. I took a tiny puff.

'Take the smoke deep into your lungs. It's such a rush.'

I jumped off the swing, the cigar between my lips. Then I fell to the ground and threw up.

* * *

A few days later, Goose said, 'Come with me. It's time.'

I followed her eight blocks to the hardware store. She took me around the back to the horse hitch. The place was empty yet smelled strongly of horse piss. Goose and I sat on an old wooden bench partially concealed by overgrown shrubs.

Before long Bush arrived. His real name was Bryan, only no one called him that. He got his nickname because of his shaggy orange hair. It was the first time I'd seen him outside of school. Bush went to the special class. He took art, social studies, and gym with us. The special class had its own kitchen, its own washer and dryer, and even its own bathroom. I knew because I delivered hot lunches there once a week.

Bush was hard of hearing. He'd had surgery but it didn't take. People had to face him when they spoke so he could read their lips. When our teacher asked him a question, something I figured anyone could answer, Bush looked away until the teacher asked someone else.

Goose elbowed me in the ribs. 'Get ready,' she said.

Bush leaned against the hitching post and flipped through a magazine.

'That's porn,' Goose said, pulling a few stray hairs from her mouth.

I wondered how she could tell what kind of magazine it was from where we were sitting. Then Goose did something weird; she undid some buttons on her blouse.

'What are you doing?' I asked.

'Wait for it,' she said.

Bush set the magazine on the ground. Next, he undid his belt. I wanted to tell Goose we should leave but part of me didn't want to.

When Bush undid his zipper and pulled down his pants, I lifted my legs and pulled them against my chest.

Goose asked, 'You okay?'

'Why did you want me to see this?' I whispered to Goose.

All she said was, 'It's time for you to grow up.'

I wondered if she'd brought anyone else here before me. But I didn't need to ask. I knew the answer. All Goose had was me; I was her only friend. Not because of the limp but because she was Goose. Independent. Strong. Unique. Opinionated. Like a tidal wave out of control.

I couldn't tear my eyes away from Bush. Goose remained next to me, each inhale of breath rattling audibly from her.

Later, when we stood up to leave, it felt like I'd maybe peed my pants.

* * *

A few years after the incident at the horse hitch, two things happened. Bush went to juvie and Goose went to the Hospital for Sick Children.

While she was there, I felt stuck. I tried to write in my diary about how much I missed her. I expected that putting down on paper a couple of lines about my feelings would make me feel better but it didn't. I found I couldn't pay attention long enough to write much so I gave up. Instead, I stood at my bedroom window, longing for her. Waiting for her to return. I begged my mom to take me to the city so I could visit her. My mom always had excuses like she was too busy or didn't have money for gas.

Goose was at the hospital for much of that semester. When I caught wind that she was back, I called her house every day asking if I could stop by, but her mom always said Goose was sleeping. The more I called, the gruffer her mom sounded. She promised to get Goose to call me when she woke up, only Goose never did.

One day Goose's mom left a message for me. 'You can come over now. Rosemarie is ready.'

I'd been waiting so long for that call. I ran to her house as fast as my legs could carry me. Goose was up in her room lying on her double bed. A giant cast covered her hips and reached halfway down one of her legs. Smudged signatures covered the plaster, names I didn't recognize. There was a trace scent of urine in the room.

Goose's face was grey and her eyes had lost their sparkle. She looked uncomfortable, as if the cast pinched. Her hair was stringy and the pink ends were split. Dark roots had grown in at the part.

I picked a stack of paperbacks off her bed and set them on the floor. I crawled in next to her, careful to not crush her. We lay like that for ages, in complete silence, like people with nothing to say.

After a while I asked, 'Want me to comb your hair?'

Goose nodded yes. She smiled as the teeth of the comb moved across her scalp.

After I'd set the comb on the dresser and lay back down, her lips brushed my hair.

'Don't ever call me Goose again,' she said. 'From now on, I only answer to Rosemarie.'

She said it so matter-of-factly. I wanted to know what had changed her mind. What had happened at that hospital? Had she had one too many surgeries? Her mom had told me that Rosemarie had been in the ICU for ten days. There had been unexpected complications after the surgery. And once she'd been released, she just didn't bounce back like the previous times. She was no longer the wild, fearless girl she had been when we had met all those summers ago.

My mother blamed everything on moods, said a teen's state of mind could change with each pulse of a metronome. Maybe that was all it was. Moodiness brought on by being a teenager. But deep down I hoped it was more. I hoped that Rosemarie was beginning to feel for me the way I felt for her, even if neither one of us knew how to talk about it yet.

I stayed next to Rosemarie the rest of that afternoon, her given name bouncing through my mind. I wondered if I'd be able to do it, to not call her Goose. And the few times that day when I forgot and the nickname slipped out, no earthquakes happened, no lightning struck from above. All afternoon I wanted to kiss her back but was scared doing so might be too much too soon. So instead, I leaned in close and inhaled the scent of her.

MISSING MIKE

A month after Rolphie was born, the skin of my breasts turned bright red and became hot to the touch. The doctor said breast-feeding sometimes causes an infection called mastitis, so she prescribed an antibiotic. Once they healed and I was nursing well again, Rolphie seemed to smell like whatever I ate.

Broccoli and asparagus made his bowels loose. A few times the diaper couldn't hold all the poo. I'd have to make a point of inspecting behind his ears and between his toes. I used a baby wipe or damp face cloth to wash him up. It seemed as soon as I had figured out how to get him completely clean, he'd fill his pants again. The creases of his neck were like pleats in those dresses my mammie made me wear to school.

I'm going over all this in my mind when I hear a commotion in the hall. I don't get up because I figure it's just a couple of Jehovah's Witnesses in search of sinners. I never tell anybody, but the truth is, I thought a lot during the pregnancy about getting rid of the baby before it got born. I suppose I'm not the first single mom to think about that. I was scared and had nobody in my court.

When I was a student at Sarnia District School there was this girl, Lydia, who also didn't seem to have anybody in her court. I can still remember what she looked like. Every day, she'd step from a white panel van parked in the turn-around in front of the school. We all thought it was weird to get driven around like that because the rest of us were walkers. On the back of the van, in bright blue letters, it said 'Morningside Homes'.

Lydia joined the gymnastics team. She sure could tumble, and her back walkovers on the beam were really good. One practice I felt sick and asked my coach to go home early. In the change room there was Lydia, rooting through my bag. She made it seem like it was okay because she had somebody's permission, but I knew she was lying because it was my bag and not somebody else's. So that's when I told her off and her face turned pale. I squealed on her and two weeks later she was gone. I wonder if she ever made the connection that she was moved for stealing from my bag, not because I ratted her out.

Anyway, I just got off the phone with family services. The courts have decided. Rolphie can't live here with me. Some would say it's better this way. My worker recommends I visit Rolphie on Sundays, but by the time I get the bus, take a transfer, and do the twenty-minute walk to where he's living, it's the end of our visiting time, so I don't bother. My worker says I haven't learned to deal with things. I don't see the problem, but she says that other moms don't do what I do. She even praises Rolphie for telling his teacher on me. Here's the thing. Nobody's got a frigging clue what it's like to live on your own, forever, with a plastic arm that hurts like a son-of-a-bitch all the time. They just don't get it.

So when it's the big day when I could go to the group home and visit, when I could be seeing Rolphie, I just sit in my kitchen and pour tea—one cup for me and one for my little Rolphie. Sometimes when I feel particularly lonely, I pour a third cup for my husband, Mike. Rolphie's dad. I imagine the two of them sitting right there in front of me, sipping from their cups, the two of them making on-purpose slurpy sounds just to make me laugh.

* * *

'Rolphie, time to come in!' Staff Lara yells.

I don't want to. I like sitting on the metal fire escape at the group home where I live now. I feel safe up here because I have the best view of the street and the sidewalk and the door, and I'm always the first to know when we have visitors.

Staff Lara usually works the evening shift. She has blond hair and is a student at the university. She's wearing tight blue jeans, slip-ons my mom calls Jesus sandals, and a T-shirt with a big red heart on it.

Earlier, over a bowl of macaroni and cheese and sliced red peppers, Lara told the four of us kids that the prime minister was in town making speeches. After dinner, Lara got me to scrape the dishes before Sanford washed them. I like Sanford. He has a cool book called *Anansi* about a Jamaican national folk hero that's actually a spider-man. The book has very colourful pictures and just a few paragraphs on each page so Sanford and I can read it without any help. Lara made Sanford wash the dishes again on account of him not rinsing the soap off well enough. She promised we could play Crazy Eights after chores. But I didn't want to so I went out for fresh air.

When they moved me to this group home, I had to change schools. I have been at my new school for thirty-three days. I keep track on a calendar Lara gave me. There are twenty-nine kids in my grade four class. We are learning to play the harmonica. I'm not very good. I forget and spit into the mouthpiece and the teacher punishes me by making me stay in at recess and help clean the musical instruments.

The teacher isn't fair and all the kids don't like her. I over-heard someone say at lunch that she picks on boys more than girls. I know this is true because I've been sliding an elastic band onto my wrist for every time I have to stand in the cloakroom. This teacher took over for the other one who left to have a baby.

Sanford told me he lives here because his mom's boyfriend liked to pick him up and shake him for no reason. This is his mom's third boyfriend who has lived with them. I don't talk about why I'm here. Talking is what got me here in the first place.

Sundays are for family visits. Every boy gets an hour. My visiting time is at 1:00. I wait in the room I share with Donovan. I watch from upstairs as he kicks a soccer ball in the backyard with his dad. He's lucky his dad comes. I don't have a dad anymore. He died before I was born. When I lived with my mom, she'd tell me about him. How I looked like him. She told me I have the same kind of nose and his dark eyes.

Donovan says every night before lights out that he's sure his dad will be coming for him the next day. But all us kids know that's not going to happen. I overheard staff say that Donovan's dad lives with another man, and that man has three of his own children. Before that, Donovan's dad neglected him and Donovan started getting picked up by the police downtown for wandering around alone.

Donovan has a couple of nasty habits. I hate listening to him clear his throat all the time. His other nasty habit is, at dinner, he eats with his mouth open so you can hear him chewing way too loudly. Other than that, he's okay.

I watch the yard some more. Staff sit on a picnic table and stare at their cellphones. When Donovan comes back upstairs, I wait for someone to call me down for my turn. I watch the red numbers on the clock. I stop watching the clock at 1:50 and roll onto my back. I rest my head against my pillow, which smells like sweat, and I stare at the ceiling, which has a circular stain on it.

* * *

I like retelling Rolphie's birth story, but most of the people at the place where I used to work have heard it already. Besides, they aren't that interested in the first place. Most people just think about stuff that concerns them, like not making the rent because they have to buy new tires or something.

One late afternoon, during the summer I still had Rolphie, I was enjoying a joint. I called Rolphie in from his bedroom and told him the part of his birth story where he was all brand new and two weeks early and covered in gunk. Rolphie perched on the edge of the kitchen chair and I could feel his nine-year-old attitude sucking the air from the room. He was doing all he could to avoid our eyes meeting. He sat up nice and tall in his chair but was doing a lot of leg squirming.

'What's the matter?' I asked. I put the smouldering end of the joint into my mouth and pushed smoke at him. Rolphie waved his hands to make the smoke go away.

I tamped the ember off and set the rest in the ashtray. 'What's gotten into you? I'm trying to have a nice quiet chat with you.'

Rolphie grunted. He wasn't ready to give a reason for why he was being so mean.

'You listening to me, Rolphie?'

He shrugged and looked away. 'I've got lots on my mind,' he said.

Despite the joint, I felt like shit. The room turned dark from the grey, shapeless clouds loafing outside the kitchen window. I thought about Rolphie having a lot on his mind. Rolphie was nine. How much stuff could he have on his mind? I remembered being nine and I never had anything on my mind.

I used a roach clip to pick up the rest of the joint I'd just toked. I lit the remains. As I exhaled, smoke surrounded Rolphie's head. I wanted to send him back to his bedroom and make him stay there for two or three days. Stay until I was sure he'd never give me attitude again. But instead I reminded Rolphie that, when he was just a little baby, I had to stop breastfeeding him for a while, despite his mouth only being the size of a raisin, because my tits hurt so bad.

'I've heard this story a million times, Mom. I just want to go out and play.'

I started to wonder what the hell was wrong with Rolphie. I read an article last week about young girls getting big breasts due to all the hormones pumped into chickens. Rolphie did seem suddenly taller than a kid his age should be. His head was big and round as a watermelon. And the more I looked at him, the more he looked like a giant cricket. I tried not to think about what would happen when the pot wore off, when the universe went back to being its usual boring self.

'I saw you looking through your dad's scrapbook again,' I said to Rolphie. 'I know how much you must miss him.'

Rolphie looked at me like I must have a second head or something and said, 'You can't miss what you never had.' And then he asked to be excused.

'Get some orange juice for me, will ya?' I said.

That's when he smirked, like he thought he was better than me. I watched him at the fridge. Nine going on fifty. He grabbed the jug and swirled the pulp around. He poured the juice all nice and careful. And then the little fucker just let the jug slip from his fingers to the floor, staring right at me all the while.

* * *

Around the corner from my mom's apartment on Peter Street is a little park. There's no playground equipment. It's not that kind of park. There's a wooden bench with green paint that has mostly peeled off. A plaque says the Family Wagler donated the bench in memory of their grandfather, Stefan. One time I did the math in my head and figured out the man lived to be over a hundred. I considered asking my mom if she ever thought of getting something in memory of my dad, but then I remembered how angry she makes me. She agreed not to smoke up when we're together in the kitchen, that she'd wait until weekends.

Mom always blamed her arm. She always says if she had a normal hand with fingers that really worked we wouldn't be in this mess.

The reason we're actually in this mess is because there's this lady who came to our school a while ago. She told us to call her Meg but I don't think that's her real name. Anyway, Meg said she used to do heroin and instead of stopping when she got arrested, she took more. Meg said heroin was better than finding a cat's eye marble in the gutter. Once, after using heroin, she found a drink umbrella on the edge of a puddle. When she opened it, thousands of umbrellas exploded out of the little one.

I remember the look on my teacher's face, how serious she got, after I told Meg and the class about me and my mom. How my teacher dialled a number on the classroom phone. How she nodded to whoever she was talking to and held her hand over the mouthpiece and whispered. How I watched the beige cord stretch and felt the hairs on the back of my neck stand up. How the teacher looked right at me, no one else. How she ordered Sonya Schwartz to watch the class while she talked in the hallway with the principal. How a stream of sweat trickled down my spine into my butt crack. I was sorry right then and there that I'd tried to impress everybody with my story about Mom smoking pot.

* * *

That same summer before they took Rolphie from me, I was sitting there in the kitchen coming down and wondering if I shouldn't try to get another nice buzz going, what with my kid with the attitude being outside and all. But I started thinking about my dead husband, Mike. After Mike died, I decided to use the second bedroom closet to grow my weed. I didn't bear in mind the danger of plugging in a frayed extension cord for the lamp I'd set up on a chair. I didn't consider how warm the bulb might get. Or that my polyester slacks hanging nearby were touching the bulb. I only thought about getting those damned plants to grow and grow fast because I wanted to dry the leaves and smoke them.

Anyway, one night I turned on the TV and there was Jerry Seinfeld. I never laughed so hard in my life. Rolphie was on the mattress in the other room. He was three or four months old. I couldn't even afford a proper crib for him. So I was just sitting there with Seinfeld blabbering on and on and my head nodded and all of a sudden something started wailing. I just sat there, listening, trying to figure out what the noise was. It didn't register for the longest time that someone was banging on my door. There was an incredible pounding behind my eyeballs.

A man was shouting, 'Lady! Your smoke detector!'

I poked the detector with the end of a broom handle to make it stop. Smoke was coming from under the closet door. I wet a face cloth and held it over my mouth and nose. I tossed blankets over the flames and stamped on the embers with my runners. I didn't consider calling 9-1-1 because I knew I'd get busted. The amazing thing, considering all the noise and commotion, is that Rolphie stayed fast asleep through the whole thing.

The burns I got on my right arm didn't seem too bad at first. I smeared them with aloe vera just like my mammie did when her arm got burned pulling pans from the oven. The skin on my arm grew ugly and tight, and it hurt so much I couldn't even stand to change Rolphie's diapers. A week or ten days after the fire, I dragged myself to emergency. It was a staph infection. The doctor asked the intern if she'd ever used bone cutters before. The first amputation took my hand. A surgeon said if I'd just come in sooner, they could have saved my hand. The second amputation took my arm to the elbow.

* * *

When I still lived with my mom, she liked to lick her fingers and tug at my cowlick. She said my dad had one just like it. Once he got so pissed off he decided to see what would happen if he shaved it off. So he did. Mom said his hair was all over the bathroom tap and sink.

When I used to look in the mirror and Mom stood behind

me, she'd tell me I have my dad's eyes. She'd say I smell just like my dad never left. That's when I'd start to miss him, which is totally nuts because I don't know how I could miss someone I've never met. He died right before I was born.

* * *

I like to page through the scrapbook I made about Rolphie's father. Some days when I try to remember Mike's face, it's so hazy I feel panic in the pit of my stomach. But then I look in the scrapbook and recall his features and feel calm again.

An old friend of mine from Sarnia District School helped set Mike and me up. We were over at her house and she had this camera on her brand new iPhone and she was shooting it all the time. I told her she should be a photojournalist. Anyway, Mike was handing me a cup of coffee and my friend said stop, and she got the camera ready and started snapping pictures and I got all embarrassed. Anyway, there was Mike, right there, bigger than life, and he was handing me the cup saying, 'Here you go.' And I was so frigging nervous and flailing my arms all over the place and wham, the coffee was in my lap and Mike's hand was there too, mopping up the spill and my friend was shooting picture after picture.

'Want to go out sometime?' Mike asked, and we were married four months later in a civil ceremony in his mom's backyard in Bradford.

* * *

Mom's apartment on Peter is only three blocks from Schneider's. She used to work there making Jumbo hotdogs and often brought home boxes of seconds. I liked it when she double-sliced the ends and fried them up. There they'd be cooking in the pan, looking all normal, and then all of a sudden they'd curl up. Mom said they looked like spider legs. She'd dip the curly parts into chili sauce and hot mustard. I'd plunge mine into BBQ sauce and gross her out by letting the sauce dribble down my chin. Mom said I should be an actor but I'm going to be a cop.

I never thought I would get Mom in trouble because I know how to roll a joint. Mom smokes when I'm around, and she needs me to roll the joints for her because she only has one hand. I remember when I got curious one time and asked if I could take a toke, too. I was sorry she let me; I couldn't stop coughing. Mom said to take a drink of milk to make the throat pain go away.

* * *

One morning I find Rolphie asleep on the floor. Sleep crusts in the corners of his eyes, the scrapbook open near his little chin, that beautiful cowlick standing straight up. It was just before the state took him from me.

Mike wasn't as good a guy as Rolphie thinks. I fight hard with myself to hide the truth about his father. A mother can't spoil her kid's fantasy of his dad, especially a dad he has never even met.

Mike always wore socks when we had sex. He was embarrassed about his toes. I wish I had a photo of him nude. I can't remember anymore what he looked like naked. I know he had a mole above his butt cheek. Now every morning when I wake up, I look at the empty pillow to my right and I say, 'You selfish fuck, Mike. You left me behind. With a kid. With a kid who's a million stars brighter than I'll ever be.'

* * *

The woman who lives in Unit 6 writes in a journal. Sometimes I invite her over for tea. She usually sits in Rolphie's chair. She says it's easy to forget the boring stuff if you don't write it down. I thought about writing a journal for Rolphie. I thought maybe I'd write about the time Mike and me went to the shooting range so he could re-qualify. He shouldn't have, but he let me shoot. He was behind me, the front of his legs pressing against the backs of mine, his hands guiding the pistol. Good thing. I was shaking so much.

* * *

The kitchen counter at my mom's place always used to be piled with dirty dishes. Pots on top of frying pans in the sink. The tap dripped. I knew my mom wouldn't want to clean the kitchen after she'd toked and I knew she'd get all sentimental and want to look at that scrapbook again. Twenty-seven, twenty-eight, twenty-nine, thirty. Thirty seconds until she exhaled.

I couldn't tell Mom that I told on her to my class. That my teacher knew she smokes pot. The class was sitting in a circle, the other kids' mouths hanging open like kids' mouths do when they are shocked by something that's been said. My teacher's white sneakers squeaked on the tiles as she sprinted around in front of us.

Sometimes I wonder. If my dad hadn't died, would any of this have happened?

* * *

I still can't believe how sensitive my husband was. Maybe you'd expect a tow-truck driver to die in a car crash of his own. But instead, right after seeing where a stupid woman wrapped her Corolla around a telephone pole, he rented a motel room and hung himself. Sometimes I kick the dresser in my bedroom. Sometimes I smoke two joints. And every day I wonder how my life could have been different.

* * *

Staff Lara tells me there was a message from the school today. I got perfect on a spelling test. We eat fish sticks for dinner, and I ask Lara when we'll have macaroni and cheese again.

Sanford is moving back with his family. Lara waited until after dinner to tell us because she didn't want us to get jealous. Lara says if my mom doesn't start to show some interest, the courts will decide to make me a crown ward. I don't know what that means except that someone could adopt me.

I remember when the judge asked if my mom was still using drugs. When she muttered, the judge told her to speak up. But that's when the air conditioner started up and I couldn't hear what she said.

I like my new life at the group home. I like playing shortstop and I can switch-hit a bit. I try not to fight too much with the other kids. Maybe one day I'll get a dad who'd like to play catch with me.

* * *

The social worker told me I'd never get Rolphie back on account of me still smoking pot. I told her instead of always pointing out what I'm doing wrong, she should work harder to get me a medical marijuana certificate.

I get so tired of people telling me what to do all the time. Nosy Parkers making such a big deal about everything. Like that social worker. When Rolphie told his teacher on me, it broke my heart because it meant Rolphie wasn't really mine anymore.

And Mike, that super-sensitive, selfish bastard! He turned my life upside-down. I was his goddamned wife and he never even thought to come home and talk to me about that woman's death. It was almost like he knew her or something. Mike's dying caused me to have to raise Rolphie all by myself. Of course I fucked it up.

My social worker says if I gave up pot, I'd learn how to feel my feelings. Only she doesn't get it and never will. Look what good Mike's feelings did for him.

HOUSE RULES

Every day Becky dragged herself out of bed around eleven. After guzzling juice straight out of the jug, she parked herself at the dining room table and began colouring inside the pre-printed lines of an adult colouring book. Today's page was emblazoned with 'Don't Tell Me What to Do' atop a field of flowers that Lydia was certain could not be found in nature.

Lydia thought the palette Becky had chosen was hideous. There was mustard yellow and cantaloupe, neon orange and lemon yellow, and an olive colour that should have been kept in a jar at the back of the fridge. They were all colours that reminded Lydia of her babysitting days: dirty diapers and baby spit-up.

Lydia wished she had established some ground rules when Becky first arrived, but she knew how much her husband, Frank, Becky's father, wanted his daughter to feel at home.

Frank still knew how to make Lydia hot. While Becky was off at school, she and Frank would make love on the top of the kitchen table or up against the front door, as if they were starring in a romantic blockbuster. They ordered in sushi rolls, something they never did when Becky was underfoot due to her intolerance of the texture of rice. Lydia missed the foot rubs while watching *Chicago Med*, *Chicago Fire*, and *Chicago PD*.

Becky was there living with them again because the university in BC had booted the students out at the beginning of the pandemic, and the job Becky had lined up for the summer had fallen through as well.

Becky had ruined everything, not that Frank noticed. But Lydia had. She took note. Now, it seemed Lydia's lot in life was to watch Becky colour all day. Outrageous! Not only was the incessant *scritch scritch* of the pencil crayons driving her mad, but the pencil shavings were everywhere, little reminders that she and Frank were no longer blissfully alone.

When the pandemic hit, Lydia and Frank had been together five years. He had shared custody of Becky with his ex-wife, but when the first lockdowns hit, his ex was heavily involved working as a researcher to develop a vaccine against the virus. She begged Frank to be flexible in the name of science. He agreed without first consulting Lydia or Becky.

Now, every morning, hunched over and ravenous, Becky emerged from her bedroom and made herself breakfast without even saying hello. While she walked through the kitchen on her way to the dining room table, she'd inhale two pieces of cinnamon toast and a banana. Then, she'd chase them down with a tumbler of milk, push her breakfast dishes aside and open the zipper on her pencil case. The sound of the zipper's teeth ripped through the Yin session with Yogi Bryan that Lydia had found on YouTube.

That girl, Lydia thought, is turning into a bulging, sagging lump of useless putty. Her only exercise was occasionally looking up from her ceaseless colouring and blinking a few times before tipping her face back towards the table. If only Becky would find something meaningful to do, like help organize the pantry, hose down the garage floor, or at the very least tidy her room.

Lydia was shocked by the girl's slothfulness, her lack of get-up-and-go. It was far worse than it had been before she'd gone off to university. She tried to talk to Frank about it but he offered an unsympathetic ear.

'She's turning into a whale right before our eyes,' Lydia complained. 'A girl her age should have girlfriends, boyfriends. When I was her—'

'At least she's making something beautiful,' Frank said.

Clowns, pirates, terrier puppies, farm scenes. As far as Lydia could see, Becky's colouring was just a short step up from a paint-by-number.

Lydia collapsed into a chair on the porch and began jotting down a list of Becky's unacceptable behaviours, and the steps that would have to be taken to rectify them immediately.

Bedroom mess	Make bed, tidy every day
Dirty hands	Wash with soap and water
Food & drinks in bedroom	Cease immediately
Music after 10 p.m.	Cease immediately
Never takes a shower	Shower every other day
Laundry piling up	Laundry days: Wed. and Sat.
Breakfast & lunch dishes	Dishwasher, wipe counter
Bathroom trash	Empty weekly

Lydia decided to share these new rules with Becky right away. She plunked the handwritten list on top of the poster Becky was trying to colour.

'Do you mind? I'm working here,' Becky said, doing nothing to conceal her sarcasm.

'Working,' Lydia scoffed. 'You haven't done a lick of work since you arrived here. All you've done is lounge around and colour your silly little pages.' She glared at the mountain of pencil shavings accumulating next to the poster. Some had already found their way onto the floor, too, and some were clinging to her socks. Insufferable!

'What's this?' Becky asked, palming the list with a grimy hand. 'You know I can't read that kind of writing.'

'Ha!' Lydia said. It was irritating that the school system didn't bother with cursive writing anymore. She prided herself on her exquisitely rendered handwriting and the flourish of her signature.

'Something for you to learn then, isn't it? Something practical instead of, instead of—' She was interrupted by the scrunch of paper as the list was mashed into a ball. She practically vibrated with simmering rage. 'Aren't there blackheads you could be squeezing?' That was Lydia's parting shot before she marched past the dining room table into the kitchen.

Lydia had once hoped that she and Becky would develop the kind of mother-daughter relationship she'd seen in magazines and on TV. They'd go on shopping trips to the outlet mall, spend weekends together in the city to take in a concert. But Lydia's stream of minimum wage jobs hadn't provided enough disposable income to actualize the fantasy, and Becky had been utterly uninterested in those outings, or in having anything to do with Lydia at all.

When Becky had moved away for school, Frank and Lydia had found themselves perfectly in sync. It had seemed almost as if he could read her mind and she his. If she was thinking of having salmon for dinner, he'd already be soaking the cedar plank. He didn't have to ask which show she wanted to watch in the evening. He just knew by glancing at her. And somehow, she knew when he was in the mood for true crime. They worked well together, like a couple of physicists with only their brains to do complex calculations.

But then the pandemic hit, and Becky had returned, parking her ass in Lydia's chair, never Frank's. Her poked-in eyes and pallid skin incited Lydia's wrath. Her turned-down mouth and constant sullenness were infuriatingly contagious.

Lydia furiously wiped baseboards and picture frames, freeing them of an imperceptible build-up of dust, stewing all the while. When she was finished, she decided to type and print out the list of MUST DOs for Becky. She settled on a legible 16-point font. She added a few more ideas to the list, like getting up by 10:00 a.m. She posted the list on the fridge door with a magnet.

'There. No excuses now!' Lydia said under her breath.

Becky's response was to drink an entire two-litre bottle of Pepsi.

Lydia stormed into the dining room. 'You stole my pop!'

'No,' Becky said calmly. 'I borrowed it.'

Lydia towered over her. 'Then give it back.'

Becky mockingly pretended to spit it up. 'It's not like I can go to the store, now, is it?' Becky sniggered.

'Well,' Lydia answered, her cheeks and neck flushing with redness, 'I guess I'm just going to have to borrow a couple of these, then.' She scanned the pencil crayons in search of the perfect colour to reflect her rising blood pressure. She plucked crimson red from the pile and snapped it in two, then another, lemon yellow this time, and another and another, until a heap of broken pencil crayons sat on the table.

'I hate you, you ice-cold bitch!' Becky screamed, storming from the room.

That night, Frank insisted the three of them try to act civil for once and watch a movie together. They couldn't agree on a genre so they played rock paper scissors to decide. Becky won and out of spite made them watch a romantic western, a genre she didn't even like.

It was close to noon the next morning when Lydia woke with a headache. She'd had most of a bottle of Merlot instead of her usual glass-and-a-half, and her mouth was parched. She popped a couple of Advil, finger-combed her unruly hair and, shielding her eyes from the light, slunk down the stairs to the kitchen.

Frank had his back to her, fiddling with the coffee maker.

'I'd like my chair back,' Lydia said hoarsely. She wasn't a tyrant; he needed to know she was willing to negotiate, to meet the girl partway. So, with both hands around her mouth for amplification, she shouted into the dining room, 'I'd like my chair back!'

All she wanted was for Frank to back her up. Was that too much of an ask?

No answer. No movement. Dead silence.

'I'm willing to bury the hatchet. It's on me to find a way to compromise. We can't go on like this.' She leaned against the door jamb to the dining room and sighed. 'I'll show her that I'm the adult here.'

The chair was conspicuously empty, the table freshly wiped, the pencils packed up, the shavings collected and in the garbage.

Lydia had trouble forming her next words. 'Frank, where —'

He turned towards her. He looked as if the air had been sucked out of his lungs. 'She's gone to live with her mother,' he said.

Lydia felt a wave of guilt and shame. 'I'm so sorry.' She pulled Frank to her and squeezed him tight. She could feel him shuddering against her chest and under her hands.

UNFOLDING RECIPES

I have an uncomplicated recipe for potato pancakes. It was my mother who taught it to me when I was young, even though my father always said he was the better cook. The potatoes came from the garden, from the small patch where my mother grew vegetables. I used to kneel on a kitchen chair and watch as she peeled the potatoes with confident, steady hands. Then, she guided each chunk of potato along the stainless steel box grater.

The grater's sharp, raised surfaces could give you a nasty cut. I remember one time my mother was careless, and droplets of blood stained the fawn-coloured potato mixture below, eventually turning it pinkish. 'Sorry about that,' she said, her voice soft and embarrassed as she studied the crimson mess in the centre of the bowl. She whistled through the gap between her top teeth while trying to scoop out the contaminated bits with a long-handled wooden spoon.

The directions were simple and clear. Once the grating was done, she dug a dollop of bacon grease out of the ceramic bowl she kept next to the stove. She scraped the hardened fat into a heated cast iron pan. She didn't refer to a recipe or use a measuring cup. She cooked by feel, relying on intuition and experience. While the fat melted, she cracked two eggs against the lip of the bowl and stirred them into the mixture she had already prepared. A pinch of salt. A handful, give or take, of finely diced onions. A few dashes of flour. A gentle squish of her fingers to combine the ingredients. Her actions seemed choreographed, her movements elegant and fluid. She was beautiful in her light blue slacks, her brunette hair gathered in a clasp at the nape of her neck, her hands dusted with flour and dripping with lumpy pancake batter.

When the fat began to crackle, she plopped blobs of batter into the pan. One, two, three, four, five. Five disks the size of her palm. She always stopped at five, for that was the right number of pancakes for one person to eat in a single sitting, no matter his or her age, size, or level of hunger. The sound of pancakes sizzling reminded me of my school's mammoth boiler, wheezing and sputtering in the halls and classrooms all winter long. The sizzles were so loud they drowned out the voices on the portable radio. Soon, puffs of smoke floated to the ceiling that had yellowed from years of cooking and a delicious, greasy smell filled the kitchen. As a child, my senses feasted on the sight, sound, and smell of my mother's potato pancakes. I could barely wait to pop one into my mouth.

* * *

In my condo, my cleaning lady keeps all the surfaces scrubbed and gleaming.

My mother bought me three small appliances as housewarming gifts: a coffee maker, which stopped working a month after the warranty ran out; a toaster, which turns bagels black no matter how much I fiddle with the setting dial; and a deep fryer, which is in the original box and sits at the back of the cupboard over the fridge.

I either go out to eat or order in. I hardly ever cook and when I do, I keep the exhaust fan turned on high. The other condo owners like it better if no strong cooking odours collect in the air.

When I eat, I stand at the counter so the crumbs fall there and not on the floor.

* * *

My mother was frying pancake batch number three by the time my father came in from the barn for dinner. Dirt coated his arms and hands, the kind of grime one gets from working on a farm and refusing to wash in the bucket of water sitting next to the back steps of the house. With each footstep he took, debris drifted to the floor. He brushed past my mother to peer into the pan on the stove before sitting at the head of the table.

'That's all we're having? A man needs meat.'

My father preferred to eat his potato pancakes with black pudding. He hankered for the combination when he and my mother moved from Germany to England after the Second World War. When I was a kid, I was stupid enough to be fooled by the name 'pudding', but this food was not dessert. It was sausage made from pigs' blood, oatmeal, and savoury spices such as mint, lemon thyme, and marjoram. Whenever my mother had a notion to fry up black pudding, I hid in my bedroom and plugged my nostrils with Kleenex.

Usually, my father sat with his body pressed against the metal edge of the table, shovelling food into his mouth like he was taking part in an eating competition, but this time, he sat far back in his seat, his hands braced wide and his face tense. He was filthy, the skin on his hands and forearms the colour of a dusty road. He smelled of sweat and chicken shit.

My mother pivoted from the stove and made a face at him. He ignored her. As she slid three pancakes, not the customary five, onto his plate, her foot collided with the leg of the table.

'What's with you?' he asked.

My mother said, 'Before you sit down, you ought to wash up already. What kind of role model are you to her?' She gestured in my direction with the frying pan. 'It disgusts me to serve good home-cooked food to people who act like pigs.'

He glared at her, and then, holding her gaze, he scraped his arm causing dirt to flick off his skin and land on the tabletop.

'That better?' he asked.

She slammed the frying pan back on the stove, tore off her apron and stomped down the hall and into the bedroom. She had turned in for the night, barely a moment past six.

* * *

My mother was prone to fits of rage and would sometimes hole up in the bedroom for days. My father loathed these episodes; he resented having to cook the meals and clean up after himself.

One time, during an episode, she asked me to go for a walk with her. I didn't have anything else to do, so I accompanied her on a stroll that took us along the slow-moving river that ran through the heart of town. We walked in silence past a pair of nesting swans, over the pedestrian bridge, past the Baptist church, to the bakery known for its mashed potato doughnuts. Back home, she set two of the doughnuts on the table in front of us, but I had to promise to eat mine quickly and never to tell my father where we'd been. There was a groove between her eyebrows. It made her look older and mean and nothing at all like my beautiful, elegant mother.

'Mom, can you be done being angry now?'

'I've found it best to resign myself to its grip on me.' Her thumb stroked a fleck of doughnut off her chin.

I had trouble seeing what she meant. I was too young, too immature and self-centred to appreciate her need for regular breaks from the roles and responsibilities of wife and mother. I took a big bite of my doughnut. The inside was bubbly soft and the outside crunchy crisp.

'Mom, remember the time I ate too many peaches and broke out in hives? The bumps were so itchy and painful you had to take me to the doctor. Is your anger like an itch that won't go away?'

'It's not like something you feel on the outside, on your skin. It's more something you feel inside, in your heart.'

'Is it like blowing up a balloon until it's so tight you know it's going to burst?'

She sighed before saying, 'Yes, it's more like that.' Her face changed then. Her cheeks flushed and her eyes turned wet behind her glasses. 'I feel like that now,' she said, collecting the dishes we'd used. 'I feel like I'm going to explode.'

I wished I had the secret antidote to rid my mother of her pain. To shape her into a parent who did consistently kind things, things I'd noticed my friends' parents do. I wanted a mother who helped me comb the tangles out of my hair. Or helped me pick out an outfit that fit properly, with patterns and colours that went together. Who cuddled with me after I'd had a rough day at school instead of expecting me to be that kind of support to her. And I longed for parents who got along, who didn't give each other dirty looks or stomp off in anger. There were times I was tempted to knock their heads together to make them love each other like I thought they should, like other kids' parents did.

* * *

I remember, after the door to the bedroom slammed, watching my father bend to scrape pancake crumbs and sour cream into the scrap bin we kept beneath the sink for the chickens. Then he wiped his fingers on his pants before heading for his lounger in the living room. He rarely slept in the bedroom with my mother. He preferred to fall asleep in his chair with the black and white TV going and a sweaty bottle of beer nestled against his crotch.

That night, and all the next day, the door to the bedroom remained closed. A narrow beam of light leaked from under it. I leaned against the door trying to feel some hint of concern for me through the thin wooden barrier. I crouched on the cold tiles and waited, willing her to rise and offer a hug. I waited there a very long time. I imagined her huddled under a heap of blankets, on her side, her knees folded against her breasts, her head resting on a pillow wet with tears.

But I'd sat like that many times before, so many times. I wondered if either of my parents would ever care enough to run their fingers through my bangs and ask me if I'd brushed my teeth or washed my hands after going pee. Slowly, very slowly, I realized I would forever be alone sitting on the tiles outside my mother's door, forever concocting a million reasons why my parents couldn't love me, their only child in the midst of a complicated home.

When my mother was in the bedroom, mornings were different, quieter, with nothing bubbling in the pan, no recipes to watch unfold. My father was too busy and hungover to do more than spill dry cereal into a bowl and set a spoon next to it. He left me to believe that the chickens needed him more than I did.

* * *

Ever since I moved away from home and into the condo, I've noticed that my mother's face has been changing. She's gone from a young mom to an old woman. She is now blind in her left eye, something to do with a detached retina. Her prominent nose looks even more so because of the deep lines around her mouth. Age spots have replaced freckles. Her jawline is fuller and puffier than before.

I'm not surprised she didn't cry at my father's funeral. I cried a lot and often, but not the kind of crying that makes a sound. I failed an entire semester because I couldn't concentrate. His swift, unexpected departure was a shock. His leaving like that left me feeling mad—not angry-mad, but the crazy kind. I'd be going to pick up pastries at the café on the way to campus and suddenly I'd spot him on a street corner or in line at the deli. I'd stand there, rooted, staring, terrified that if I blinked, he'd slip away or be swallowed by a storm sewer.

When I think about my father, I try to remember the rare times when he opened up to me. Showed me a friendly, happy side of himself. He used to wave me over and invite me to squeeze into a small spot he left open for me on his chair. We'd watch *The Price is Right* together and giggle at how silly the contestants were. He always said the show's producers ought to select him to appear on the program, that his antics would make the studio audience burst out laughing.

But mostly when I look back, I remember that my parents put me in a tough place for a child. That I had to take on the role of referee, with no choice but to wedge my tiny body between them to try to break up their fights. Perhaps if I had known then why they were so angry at each other, I wouldn't have spent so much of my childhood blaming myself for their arguments. Maybe if I had known, I would now be able to make my mother's potato pancakes without gusts of anger rising up inside me until I feel like a balloon blown up to the point of bursting.

I've got a good job now, and I've been living on my own in my condo for almost ten years. My cleaning lady keeps the place spotless. When I return to the old kitchen to visit my mother, the smell of bacon grease and the sight of the oily yellow ceiling make me nauseous. I suppose I'm not used to so much fat in my diet anymore. Like I said, mostly, I either go out to eat or order in.

FACTITIOUS

Rain on the kitchen window. Hundreds of islands dot Georgian Bay, but on this Saturday morning in August, a curtain of mist shrouds them from view. It's a day designed for unearthing dust bunnies from beneath the couch and mopping floss spittle off mirrors. But, instead, I turn on my laptop and reread an old Facebook message from Caitlin—my co-worker and friend.

Hey Toby,

I had the dry heaves again last night. I thought once radiation was done, I'd stop barfing. The tattoos itch like a son-of-a-bitch. You know how I hate to swear.

I put an update on that online site *Bridges of Caring* and got seventeen hits before bedtime. Have you ever typed your own name into Google? Try it. I stopped reading after seeing thirty references to yours truly. It's reassuring to think that so many people actually seem to care.

I wish I could talk to my birth father about my sickness. He'd be able to tell me if it's the same form of neuroblastoma I had as a kid. I don't recall having radiation treatments then. You'd think I could remember something important like that.

When I had childhood cancer, I used to write in a diary. My oncologist suggested it. But then my diary burned in that house fire, the one I told you my foster brother set. Haven't been back to Sturgeon since.

I've been thinking about updating my websites. *Bridges of Caring* doesn't take too long, but the entries I write for *Kids with Cancer Again* and *Sick Kids Unite* are seriously time-consuming. Let's face it—those sick children need me.

Anyway, got to go flush my IV lines. I should be able to stop having two drips next weekend, but who knows what else might pop up in the meantime. I'll see what my medical team suggests.

Write when you get a chance.

C!

Something has been preventing me from responding to her message. I've already taken several stabs at it. Last week I managed to write a brief answer to her question, admitting I'd never considered looking up my name on the Internet. Perhaps if I had, I'd have realized sooner that Toby is a unisex name, a shortened version of Tobias, and that many people who knew me only by name might assume I was a man. The fact is, other people's lives offer greater appeal than my own.

I also told her about a dream I had where I was trapped inside a whale. I kept jabbing it from the inside until it finally spit me out. The inside of the whale was slimy, smelly, and super scary. I woke with a start, clammy all over and afraid for my future. I wrote out the whole experience for Caitlin, but when I reread it, it sounded stupid, so I deleted everything.

I used to be a size fourteen until Caitlin came into my life. Now I wear a ten. Even my shoes are roomier, and I sure never predicted that would happen.

Caitlin taught me how to avoid extra calories. She said to eat slowly and then excuse myself before the end of a meal and head for the bathroom. 'Push a finger down your throat until you have no choice but to hurl. Two fingers work better than one. Remember to flush the toilet so no one hears.'

Ronnie doesn't like me so skinny. He says I look sick. He mentioned last week that we seem to be going through a lot more toilet paper than usual and he is, of course, correct. It's those laxatives Caitlin got me onto.

A granola bar wrapper sits beside my coffee cup. I pick it up to read the calorie count. Ninety calories and one gram of fat. I force myself to take another nibble before I tap on the keyboard.

Dear Caitlin,

I know. That 'dear' is so formal. But what the hell, it's how I feel about you and it's been way too long since I last wrote. You'd be the first to kick me for being down on myself; I shall avoid self-deprecation. I downloaded a free dictionary app and I see that self-deprecation is the word of the week. The ads on the app are annoying so I'm considering coughing up $1.99 for the ad-free version.

Ronnie has been such a prick again. I'm very familiar with your thoughts on Ronnie. He wouldn't like that I'm writing to you. It's not like I've got so many friends that I can just throw one away. I feel I can't talk to Ronnie anymore. Like you used to say, men are only interested in two things: blow jobs and sports.

I'll admit you've been crowding my thoughts. It's unlike you to not be in touch, and, besides, you wouldn't believe the rumours. A girl at work contacted Human Resources to ask if they knew where you were, but with the privacy rules being so strict, HR wouldn't say. So, I'm asking. Where the hell are you? I called your niece to see if she's heard from you. I left three messages but she hasn't bothered to call back.

Since you've been gone, I've been showing signs of coming unglued. Last week, I stood in the grocery store clutching a cart and I couldn't move. It was like my feet were frozen to the floor of the produce section. I stood there staring at the watermelons until I started counting them out loud. Then I remembered I needed tomatoes. I kept counting those goddamned melons while stacking a million vine tomatoes into the cart.

The produce manager tapped me on the shoulder. 'Everything okay here?'

The little tomatoes kept slipping through the cart and splitting open when they fell to the floor.

'Do you know that your tomatoes smell mouldy?' I said.

Sure, my voice was loud by then, and it didn't help that the manager had grabbed my elbow. I managed to pull away and found myself behind the steering wheel of my car. It felt like someone had fastened a bowline knot around my chest. I clutched the wheel and almost ran over somebody while driving out of the parking lot. In the meantime, a chain of bruises sprouted along my arm.

On the way home I spun the dial on the radio and heard the announcer saying, 'Missy Masterson, aged 93, resting at Earl's Funeral Home. Visitation Sunday afternoon. Lorne Lachine, aged 88, no funeral or visitation. Predeceased by his wife, Verna, and daughter, Elsbeth.' I waited for the announcer to say my name only he never did. Ronnie mustn't ever know about this.

Remember when you lost your hair? You had the thickest, blondest curls. Did your lashes ever grow back? Your bald head looked like you'd waxed it. Your head has that perfect shape; you never had to bother with a headscarf and it took forever to get that special wig made.

Strangers are such snoops! They'd go right up to you and start asking what you had. And you'd smile that gorgeous smile and answer with more detail than most of us could. Like when we were at Coffee Culture and, sick as you were, you held the door for that guy in the wheelchair. I remember he had a robot voice when he asked you. Throat cancer, you said. It was kind of weird considering you actually had neuroblastoma, but you probably didn't want to tell some random guy in a coffee shop all your private business.

Remember when Marita set up that website so everyone could share their thoughts and well wishes? I was so pissed because, well, it should have been me who did that. We're besties, after all.

Sometimes when you talk about your cancer, you sound like a doctor. You've got that incredible memory for scientific words. Maybe you should think about finishing high school. Lots of people return to school later in life. Maybe when you're feeling better. I have to say, your energy level is unsettling. Anyone else I've known with cancer is hunched over the toilet, but not you.

I see *Bridges of Caring* has over 21,000 followers. Frankly I think it's those photos you post. The one of you at your stepsister's house is particularly touching, both of you wearing masks because you were afraid of catching a virus. She rented that special hospital bed and placed it in her living room so you wouldn't be stuck at Mill River Health Centre. She arranged for that practical nurse, but you cancelled at the last minute, saying you could manage your own chemo port. Nothing about needles freaks you out. The video with you in the oxygen mask is a bit blurry. I mean, I know it's you. And those gasping noises—no one can keep a dry eye after watching that. To think you almost died.

Last week I called your stepsister to ask about you, but she hasn't returned my call either.

Remember when you baked that double batch of muffins for the staff? You had just picked the blueberries and everything. Your get-up-and-go is astounding. You credit the vitamin D supplements and the iron shots from the naturopath, but truthfully, you are simply an amazing woman.

Love you always,
Toby

P.S. I'm coming right back to write more. I just remembered I have to let the dog out.

I stretch out my lower back and do a few shoulder rolls. The fog has lifted and the rain has mostly stopped. I go upstairs and let Daisy out into the backyard for her first pee of the day. She pauses after every step as if to say *really?* to the idiot who tossed her out in bad weather. Blackbirds call from the hedge that runs between our house and the neighbour's. I pour a second coffee before letting Daisy back in. She jumps onto her cushion by the window, circles three times and groans before settling down for a nap. I take a sip of coffee before heading back to my laptop.

Dear Caitlin,

Part II

After your chemo last spring, I couldn't resist booking that trip to Cancun for us. You begged me to let you pay, but I wouldn't hear of it. Ronnie says only a loser would get sucked into such an arrangement. The fight that followed lasted a week.

Most patients drag someone along to the cancer clinic but not you. You're so brave. You always resisted my offers to go and sit with you. You said I'd get bored and I get that. After dropping you off, I'd head over to the park to feed the squirrels. Later, you'd be out front, finished well before expected. You said it was because you had cooperative veins, but I think you charm the hospital staff with that brilliant smile of yours.

Remember that time I took you to Pearson Airport so you could catch the red-eye to Philadelphia? That was the day we got the unexpected spring snowstorm. I was terrified to drive and, truth be told, I should have cancelled, but I just couldn't bear to see the disappointment on your face. And after that four-and-a-half-hour white-knuckle drive all the way from Wiarton, we finally got to the airport and you never said a thing; no 'thanks' or 'see you' or anything. When I offered to go in and wait with you, you waved me off. I thought it best to stick around in case the flight got cancelled on account of the storm, but you insisted you didn't need me, so I left. I followed a Challenger transport truck much of the way home.

Mae from work cornered me a week after the Philly trip. We were on break and I was in the washroom washing my hands. Mae stood over me as I held my hands under the dryer and air-tapped my shoulder in that bossy way she has. 'I want to talk to you about Caitlin,' she said.

'No one having chemo could possibly find the energy to write a speech, travel overnight, and speak to two hundred people. I'm telling you, there's something about her that doesn't sit right.'

But, here's the thing. Mae brought up a good point so I have to ask. How did you make out in Philly?

I am terrified of running into Mae, so now I use the second-floor washroom. I recently read an article about introverts in a magazine. The writer says quiet people have to spend time getting all their facts straight before they can dredge up the courage to speak. People like me, the article says, have got great ideas but lack confidence. Not like extroverts who blurt something out just to hear their own voices.

An assertive person would have stood up to her. I know you wouldn't have taken her crap.

Last week I felt safe refilling my plastic water bottle at the fountain in the corridor because I'd heard Mae was off sick. Turned out she only took the morning off. That's how she was able to creep up behind me.

'About that friend of yours, that Caitlin. The girls and I have been talking. We think she's got what they call factitious disorder.'

I didn't say anything right away. I listened for other people, but all I heard was the clack of the photocopier from that room off the hallway. Instead of looking at Mae's face, I trained my eyes on the top of her right ear.

I took a deep breath and thought about what you would do. Then I exhaled slowly and it felt like a rope wrapped around my chest had suddenly loosened. I said, 'Here's the thing, Mae. Caitlin is my friend. You're standing here like a big ole detective, demanding proof of what you say are lies. I don't have a single thing to add.' Well, you should've seen Mae's face. It turned in on itself like a deflated balloon.

Mae's word-of-the-week: factitious. It's on my list of words to look up on the dictionary app.

Here's hoping I'll hear from you soon.

Love, Toby

I hit enter. As the message flashed away, fatigue gripped me and I realized I'd spent way too much time writing to someone I wasn't certain would answer.

Suddenly I remembered that time at Coffee Culture when Caitlin had just hurled a mouthful of sushi and this guy at the next table lit up a joint and offered it to her. He said he had early-onset MS and that pot helped alleviate nausea. Then the topic switched to Caitlin and before I knew it, this guy with MS and another couple who were sitting nearby started oohing and ahhing about her cancer and I remembered just wanting to crawl home. It wasn't the first time Caitlin had demanded the spotlight, nor would it be the last. I suppose I just wasn't in the mood for grandiose infusions of Caitlin every time we were together.

Mae and her gang at work had tried to shine doubt on Caitlin, but there was nothing any of them could say to make me suspicious of my friend. I'd been there during Caitlin's darkest moments. I'd wiped her face and the back of her neck once she'd arrived home after chemo. She'd always complain of feeling sweaty and grimy after the chemicals went through her system. I helped her choose a new makeup palette to brighten up her skin tones. That's what friends do. They support each other, no matter what.

ENTANGLEMENTS

'This is the last time. Pay attention or I'll have no choice but to hand you your walking papers,' the head waiter growled, demonstrating the proper way to set a table. Ben had been placing flatware and napkins on too much of an angle.

The head waiter impatiently watched Ben's progress for a few moments before striding across the dining hall toward the floor-to-ceiling windows. Whitecaps formed on the lake under a brooding indigo sky. The last of the motorboats had docked well ahead of the brewing storm, the fifth one to hit in as many days. Gulls rocked in the waves, glaring at the fishermen, another disappointing day on the water etched on the men's faces as they trudged to their cabins.

Ben placed squares of butter into bowls of crushed ice and reflected upon his decision to leave high school to take this job at the fishing lodge. Situated on an island miles from his Etobicoke home, he was isolated by more than the lodge's remote location. No Internet. No cell service.

After Ben and his girlfriend, Carla, dropped out in mid-April, they'd bummed around his house until his father stumbled upon a pants-less Ben on top of Carla in the living room. His tense body towered over Ben and Carla as they scrambled to get dressed. 'Find a job or I'll take you down to the shop and put you in charge of power washing the septic tank trucks,' he growled.

A few weeks later, Ben and Carla headed off in his second-hand hatchback to a pair of hospitality jobs they'd seen advertised by a resort north of North Bay. Admittedly, it wasn't quite what they'd expected. The 'resort' had obviously seen better days.

Inclement weather and lousy fishing left the guests foul tempered and long-faced. Ben felt like he had to tiptoe around them, worried he might say something stupid to set them off. What if he got fired? He was desperate for money, but more than that, he wanted to prove he wasn't the lazy good-for-nothing his dad thought he was.

Carla got hired as a chambermaid. Once the novelty of the lodge wore off, she couldn't stop griping about the place. 'The uniform clashes with my eyes,' she moaned. 'And if another jerk leaves his boxer-briefs on the floor, I'll drown him in the lake.'

'The contract is only three months. We've already pretty much got a month out of the way. We can do this,' Ben said, giving her a weak smile. 'Look, I've been keeping a tally of our earnings on the wall by the door.'

She shrugged like she didn't give a damn.

While at the lodge, Ben had hoped to rekindle an interest in fishing again. He'd overheard mention of a large school of walleye spotted on some of the anglers' fish finders. In his opinion, walleye were the best eating fish out there. Moist white flesh. Easy to clean. No overly fishy taste like trout.

Perhaps he could entice Carla into taking an interest. He could teach her how to cast from shore. But he felt he should wait to ask her when she was in better spirits.

When Ben was a child, maybe eight or nine, he and his dad used to go on week-long fishing expeditions. Ben soon mastered how to bait a hook so the worm would wiggle and jiggle, how to tie a leader, the correct way to reel in a catch, and how to land a fish. He missed those outings. They were a chance for the two of them to bond over a campfire, roast marshmallows, and test out new equipment. It had been his father who had taught Ben the best way to filet a fish so that the bones did not end up in the flesh.

The last couple of hours of their fishing trips together were often tense. The furrow between his father's eyes would deepen and he would raise his voice for Ben to hurry up and pack his gear so they could miss the heavy traffic on the trip home. Once he threatened to leave Ben behind if he didn't get the fishing equipment and camp-stove stored properly in the trunk. When his father's business doubled in size, the outings ground to a halt. Ben hadn't felt as close to his father as a result.

Being off grid wasn't something Ben and Carla had counted on. Mail arrived on Tuesdays and Fridays, and neither had received any. Carla prayed for a letter, something to let her know that her friends and family back home still cared. And Ben was surprised that his dad, busy as he was, hadn't popped a postcard into the mail.

'I miss being able to catch a movie at the Paramount. I miss Netflix. Just when I finally get off shift thinking I'm done for the day, I get told to haul my ass into the kitchen to help with the dishes. It sucks. I hate this place!' Carla said, flopping onto the mattress of the cabin they shared.

Last week she finally managed to book a few hours off, and Ben hoped they might spend the time relaxing together and rekindling their romance. He swept the floor, made the bed, and wiped down the bathroom so she wouldn't have to. Instead, she headed for the trail that snaked its way around the back of the island. When she returned she was a different person. There was a buoyancy to her step and her cheeks had a tinge of colour in them. She claimed walking helped her work out her temper.

It certainly didn't help their relationship that the cabin was small, the mattress lumpy, and the lights too dim. Most of the dresser drawers stuck, and there wasn't enough space for one person's clothes, let alone two. And it pissed Carla off that they were forced to sit and eat on uncomfortable twig furniture on the narrow, screened-in porch.

'Couldn't you see if there's something else—a cabin with a tub instead of a shower?' she asked Ben one night. The next day, Ben dutifully asked the owner, who told him that sort of accommodation was reserved for the paying guests.

When Carla started whining, it got so Ben couldn't stand the sound of her voice. All he wanted to do was make love and keep Carla happy. He didn't get what her problem was. He liked the lodge, the quick access to the outdoors, and even the customers. Most of them were fly-in Americans, so they had money to throw around, and he'd caught on to the tipping protocol. If he showed his tables attention no matter how dull their stories, if he genuinely listened, the guests would gladly mine their wallets for fives and tens. Dining room work was steady, so the shifts flew by. He was a sucker for the natural surroundings and the freshwater lake. He liked to sprawl on a rock in the evenings, listening to the call of the loons. In the morning he loved how the trees floated in the mist.

On the walls of the lodge were taxidermied fish caught years before when walleye and even largemouth bass were still consistently biting. Next to the fireplace were photographs of anglers, mostly men, holding their catches on fish stringers. Tattered maps of the area, hot fishing spots represented by red plastic pushpins, hung next to the photographs. A yellowed paper listing the anglers and the date and year of their catch was taped next to the maps.

Ben wanted to be able to add his name to that list. And Carla's, too.

But the day Ben and Carla had arrived at the lodge, the fishing had gone from mediocre to dreadful. Only the couple from Oriole Cabin had managed to net a pair of walleye and, even then, the fish were scrawny. The dining room guests had begun good naturedly mocking Ben for the dismal fishing—as if he had any power over the fish and their attraction to the bait or lure on offer.

Ben hoped for a day or two of storm-free weather so he could carry out proper fishing technique, the way his dad had taught him. The boathouse even had some gear he'd been told that staff could borrow during their breaks. Perhaps he could share some fishing tips and strategies with the clientele. But when he shared his plans with management, Ben was told that, as a first-year lodge employee, instead of pining to become a fishing guide he should concentrate on his dining room duties. He would have to prove himself before looking for other things to do with his time.

One afternoon during his break, Ben headed back to the cabin to check on Carla. She'd complained of feeling poorly that morning, said she'd had cramps and lower backache. As he made his approach, he felt his mood shift. It was as if someone had slipped a shroud over his head. He wished he knew what was in store for him inside the cabin, but lately, that was *the* big unknown. The constant rain didn't help. By the time his foot hit the steps, his shirt was soaked and his mood was dark.

He pulled open the cabin door to find Carla curled up in bed, crying. He felt helpless to console her. He simply folded her into his arms and patted her hair, whispering that everything would be fine; there was nothing to worry about.

'Needed the afternoon off again?' he said when she calmed.

'You're wet,' she said, shrugging him off.

He pulled off his top, mopped his chest, back, and arms with a towel, and buttoned on a dry shirt.

'I had a terrible dream,' Carla said, her voice soft but mopey. 'Our cabin lifted off in the wind and got tossed into the lake. I ended up in some driftwood on the shore. Seagulls were pecking at my face.'

Ben had never been good at soothing distress. His mother had been overrun with fears his whole life: spiders, the dark, heights, drowning, being assaulted. But Carla's moaning and groaning about some dream, actually curling up in bed and crying like she had, seemed to him complaining for complaining's sake. 'That's horrible, babe,' he said awkwardly. He made himself comfortable on the bed next to her and continued rubbing her back. 'You do know that these cabins would never budge. They're bolted to bedrock. And besides, the lodge has been here since forever.'

Ben didn't think Carla's dream was so bad, really. He had dreamed about seagulls many times before. He found the birds to be soothing, freeing, as if their ability to soar through the sky represented a release from his own worries. Though fighting off their pecking beaks, he agreed, would be frightening. And wind was power and strength, and yes, sometimes destruction, but it was also change: warm breezes colliding with cold air, resulting in a shift in weather. During their trips to the lake, his dad had taught him the importance of watching for changes in wind direction when they were out on the water. A sudden switch could spell tragedy for boaters.

'Maybe a walk with me might do you some good,' Ben said. 'Try your hand at fishing.'

'In the rain? In the goddamned incessant rain?' Carla asked, rolling over to face him, her brow furrowed, one eye shrinking to the size of a dime. Sadness poured from her as if from an open faucet.

What his dad had done, when his mother got overwhelmed and decided to hole up in their bedroom for days on end, was head for the office, even if it was a Saturday. He'd order takeout to be delivered to the house for Ben and his mother and KFC or pizza for the office. His dad even kept a cot folded up behind his desk so he could sleep there. While Ben felt powerless to help Carla out of her funk, he refused to run away as his father had.

'I don't know how much longer I can do this,' Carla sobbed. 'I hate it here. Yesterday another employee put salt in my coffee and everybody laughed when I spit it all over the place. The guests' cabins smell like farts. And ours is even worse. It's got a mouldy smell. And I hate never being able to take a bath. You have to get me out of here.'

Ben was tempted to say she could go jump into the lake, but he thought better of it. 'Want me to warm you up some milk?' he asked instead.

'I don't want any goddamn warm milk!'

Ben watched her hands and the shaking as she bent over to light a cigarette.

The size of the cabin affected them both, but in different ways. Tiny as it was, it was bigger than Ben's room back home, and it had a few amenities. There was an electric kettle, a microwave, and a mini-fridge. Ben poked around the shelves, taking note of the bag of spoilt lettuce, some cheese slices, a couple of cans of beer, salami, and a half-empty carton of milk. It wasn't much, but the lodge owner promised to do a grocery run to the mainland after the weekend.

When Ben and Carla first arrived, they'd tossed a coin to see who'd be making food for the two of them. When Carla lost, Ben had felt relieved. He'd believed that since his job was physically more taxing, it was only right that Carla cook the meals. Only now it didn't look like she'd be making much of anything before he had to go back on shift. He'd have to see what he could scrounge from the kitchen.

He moved to leave, and Carla stamped out her cigarette before twisting up from the bed with her back to him, a position that confirmed she was still in a state. He bent down to kiss the back of her head, but she stiffened under his touch.

He pulled her to him anyway. 'My shift's starting. You going to be okay?' he asked.

'Just feeling a little off,' she said. Her face was blotchy, the pillowcase wet. This, Ben thought, was so not like her. She was usually a soft, dreamy sort of girl who sang as she solved math equations—or at least she had been here up until the two of them ditched their textbooks for jobs. He couldn't remember anymore whose idea it had been to quit school.

He ran his fingers through her hair once more before heading back to the lodge to start his shift. The rain had stopped, but lightning still flashed outside the dining hall. Guests began to file in for supper, but thoughts of Carla filled Ben's mind. It had been her idea to apply at the lodge. There were jobs in and around Etobicoke, but she'd insisted this was a chance at adventure. The employment centre had encouraged her. *Think of the money,* the counsellor had said. *The lodge offers free room and board, so you can save every cent you make!*

As Ben finished filling glasses with water, he wondered how Carla had managed to avoid getting fired. She'd been taking more time off, or not completing her scheduled shifts, but she never got in trouble with the management. Ben, more than anyone, knew how sexy she was, and felt a flash of jealousy thinking the owner probably had the hots for her.

Mr Saunders from Cormorant Cabin started griping to Ben about getting stranded on the other side of the island after flooding the engine of his boat. Tom and Jeanine had gotten themselves turned around in some of the back bays and ended up having to launch a distress signal. Ben began to wonder how much lamenting he'd be able to put up with.

After the supper rush, Ben returned to the cabin to get his smokes. The lodge didn't approve of servers keeping cigarettes on them. Carla was out. Good. Maybe she was trying to get her shit together. The fridge door was open. She'd left a note. *Eat up!* What the hell did that mean? He lit a cigarette and opened the windows to air the place out. Maybe it would help get rid of the mouldy smell Carla complained about.

Back in the dining hall, Mr Saunders and Tom were battling it out over who had the best fish story. Ben collected the half-dozen empty beer bottles that sat on the table between the men. Every time Mr Saunders knocked the heel of his fist against the table for emphasis, Tom tipped his chair onto its two back feet, as if to avoid his dinner companion's boastfulness.

'I've got a good one for you,' Mr Saunders said, gripping the edges of the table to prevent himself from wobbling. 'There's that time I cast a leech against Granite Point. The bait's not in the water more than five seconds when the line starts stripping off the reel. I yell, "I've got a big one!" But it turns out it's just a snag. I hook a new leech on and cast again in the same spot. A minute hasn't gone by when the line starts screaming again, the pole doubles over, and I'm certain I've hooked a monster. I start worrying if I'll be able to get the bugger into the boat.'

'Sounds like you had a Muskie.'

'Sure as shit felt like one. Anyway, the line goes quiet again, so I lean over and peer into the water.'

'You're lucky the bugger didn't pull you in.'

'Right? Know what it was?'

'A boot?'

'No, you idiot. Two fishing poles entangled with a log!'

'All this time waiting and *that* was your big story? Jesus!' Tom stood and stretched his arms overhead, his long fingers brushing the ceiling tiles.

'Actually I have another—'

'I'm not in the mood for any more of your overblown yarns. I'm going back to the cabin to take a nap.' The screen door slammed shut behind Tom.

The story niggled at Ben. He felt terrible for Mr Saunders. He knew what it was like to try and do your hardest to impress a man disinclined to give credit where credit was due. He was certain that, with his skills and experience, he could find a fish big enough to shut Tom right up. With a couple of hours left before it turned dark, he decided to try his luck and see if he could hook something halfway decent. Maybe a largemouth bass. Or perhaps a walleye.

With the rain dried up and the winds gone, conditions were ripe. He leapt along the rocky trail down to the boathouse to grab some gear and a few baby leopard frogs as bait. He headed for the bay off the north end of the island where there was great rock structure and plenty of weeds—it was a perfect hiding place for wary fish.

Ben carefully poked a hook through the jaws of the frog. After a few short practice casts, Ben started to feel his fishing stride return. As his index finger cradled the line, he detected a slight movement from the frog. It was pumping its legs along the surface of the water, kicking like an Olympic swimmer.

All of a sudden, the pole bent in half. Felt big, whatever it was, doubling back and forth trying to worm its way free. Ben set the hook and then alternated between reeling and pulling, giving the fish time to wear itself out before he landed it on shore. Once it was out of the water, Ben set it against a rock and crushed the skull beneath his heel, leaving the fish to tremble one last time before resting in silence. A good-sized walleye. There were more where it came from, but Ben only needed the one. He hooked a thumb and finger through the walleye's gill and took a selfie. He wouldn't be able to post the picture for his dad to see until he had reliable WiFi, but the dead fish was all the proof he needed at the fish camp.

He swung by Mr Saunders's cabin. He was on the porch, a can of beer wedged between his knees, his bare feet on the railing. Ben held up the fish. 'After that lame story you told, it seems you need this fish more than I do.'

Mr Saunders narrowed his eyes and held up a hand. 'I can't take your fish, son.'

'I wish you would. I know what it's like to not measure up.'

Mr Saunders nodded solemnly. 'I'll think about it.'

'If you want, I can show you and Tom and Jeanine, if she wants to come, where I hooked it,' Ben offered. 'You could catch your own big fish. It'll be a great story.'

'Heard they're leaving. Fed up. Hopping the water taxi bright and early after breakfast.'

'So you'll take the fish?' Tom asked, holding up the walleye one more time.

'I'd better not, son,' Mr Saunders said, giving Tom a wide smile. 'I've been coming to this lodge for over thirty years. Think of the hit to my reputation if people learned a server had to catch my fish for me.'

The lodge cook agreed to clean Tom's fish and fry it for him to eat after the lodgers finished their breakfast in the morning.

Back at the cabin, Ben found Carla already in bed, her back to him. He slid under the covers and snuggled against her.

'I caught a fish. We can have it for breakfast tomorrow, if you want.'

Her body stiffened. 'Do you mind? It's my time of the month,' Carla said, folding into herself.

* * *

The next morning, the lake was choppy but navigable. Blue patches overhead promised better fishing. Once the last of the guests had left the dining hall for their boats, Ben headed for the cabin, a plate of fish in hand for Carla. In the moist air, he could hear the water taxi's engine revving. Ben turned and squinted at the marina. Tom and Jeanine and all their gear were there. Carla was there, too, her hand resting on the arm of a dockhand, her bags on the dock beside her.

THE DOMESTIC LIFE OF A PICKER

Liliana wears sneakers over a pair of wool socks she picked out of
the clothing bin at Duke and Main. She's elbow-deep in a pile of
used clothes in the lean-to at the back of the house. The bare
bulb dangling overhead makes the small space toasty. She pushes
the sleeves of her mauve sweater halfway up her arms. The
sweater is a lucky find, too, like the Levi's she's wearing. She
hasn't bought new for years. She sifts through the pile, scrutiniz-
ing for quality and size. It doesn't pay much, but she likes being a
picker because she can make her own schedule. All she has to do is
raid the city's donation bins and rate the contents. She sells her
finds to a guy who pays her under the table.

Liliana's biceps are smooth, her hands strong and capable.
She's a vintage seeker on the hunt for shredded denim, camou-
flage hunting gear, striped T-shirts, long-sleeved tops with a cos-
mic feel, and those leather jackets with off-centre zippers that are
all the rage in Japan.

She shares the rent with three male artists. When the weather
is fair, the men put their creative pursuits on hold so they can kick
a ball around in an abandoned lot down the street. They slather
their skin with sunblock before heading out, but they aren't the
sort to stretch their muscles before or after playing.

This November they've had to put their tomfoolery on hold.
It's been a particularly gloomy month, with non-stop concrete-
coloured skies and daytime temps hovering around freezing. During these bleak days the artists feel inspired to remain inside and

make art. Liliana has been the target of their creative endeavours. They paint portraits of her, and there are charcoal sketches of her most desirable asset, namely her butt, all over the house.

A mid-morning program about culture and entertainment plays on the portable radio Liliana keeps beside the sorting table. She abhors listening to music while she works but loves talk radio, and she will keep a program on even if the topic is music.

One of the artists buzzes her on the phone to remind her that it's time to take a break. Translation: they need her inside to prepare their mid-morning snack.

She walks past wilted dahlias to the screen door. She is never certain who will be home. The artists who live with her are men she sleeps with or has in the past. In fact, at one time or other, she had been married to two of them. Sometimes her exes still crawl into bed with her, more often to sleep than to roll around under the covers.

She slips off her sneakers and sets them by the door. Her former husbands are talking about whatever artists talk about.

After a while she interrupts. 'Where's Newt?'

'Taking a dump,' the exes say together, their words perfectly synchronized.

'Anyone offer to help him out?'

'I'm surprised you even noticed he wasn't here. You've been so preoccupied with work,' Gerry, her second husband and most recent ex, says. If asked, Gerry would admit he enjoyed connecting with Liliana at mid-morning break if only to point out her character flaws.

After placing slices of buttered banana bread on a platter, she turns toward Bill, ex-husband number one. 'How come you're up so early, Bill? No reruns on the tube last night?'

While Liliana and Bill were married, he had often kept her up all night with his non-stop channel clicking and incessant humming. He had a passion for police dramas. She finally divorced him because he tended to fall asleep partway through an episode, culminating in a cacophony of snoring and farting from his side of the bed.

'You make the best damn banana bread in the whole wide world,' Bill says, his mouth full and grinning.

Occasionally the artists sell something, but their work doesn't tend to fetch much in the way of interest or income. After they adjust for costs, there's very little left to put into the savings jar. Once in a while, in return for a pretty good fee, Gerry gives feisty lectures at the local community centre on how to reignite one's artistic mojo.

The artists recently claimed the living room as their studio. Their creations, in various stages of completion, sit on the sofa, sprawl on the end tables, and hang from their easels. Liliana doesn't think the art is any good. She especially doesn't care for Bill's sculptures, which are constructed from crushed dog food cans snatched from the neighbours' recycling.

Truth be told, she's not what you'd call a supporter of visual art. Not that she has anything against it; there are simply other things in life more deserving of attention, such as getting a tune-up for her rusty old truck. Yet, no question, she prefers visual art over music. She refuses to shop in some stores because of what they're piping out of their speakers.

The current commune-like atmosphere of the house was Gerry's fault. One day, months after their breakup, as they'd sat under the linden tree in the backyard with a bag of grapes and a container of cheese curds on the picnic table between them, Gerry had revealed his plan to start an artistic community, a place where like-minded individuals could live together and create.

'I need people to bounce ideas off of,' he'd said, his eyes begging her to say yes.

'Who do you have in mind, specifically?' Liliana had asked, her lips pursing.

Gerry's grunted response should have clued her in to the fact that he had been up to something. Later that night, probably right after dinner, once she'd left to check out the donation bin out in a nearby strip mall parking lot, Gerry had hacked her Facebook account and combed her contacts. He had quickly zoned in on Bill, her first husband, and Newt, a recent but former lover she'd met after her divorce from Gerry. He'd recognized the names because of her relationships with them.

When Liliana had come home the next morning after a night of dumpster diving, Newt and Bill had already moved themselves in. 'Are you crazy, Ger?' she had shouted. 'My first ex-husband and my former lover? You must have shit for brains.'

Liliana couldn't help but feel blindsided by Gerry foisting the arrangement on her. She should never have trusted him. After all, they had met during one of her dumpster dives on the edge of High Park. When she pulled out what looked like a brand-new leather jacket, he claimed he'd accidentally dropped it into the bin and needed it back.

It wouldn't have been easy to send the guys packing. They'd already made themselves at home. And who could resist their cute baby bird faces nodding up and down every time she placed food in front of them?

The more she thought about it, the more she believed there were aspects to the living situation that might offer benefits. So she had let it go, and she could admit to herself now that the current state of affairs had its good points. The men provided her with people to talk to, and sleeping with them once in a while only strengthened their relationship, twisted them together like pieces of twine.

Bill had proposed to Liliana right out of high school. They had been little more than children when they eloped and left their small town on the peninsula and headed for the city so he could attend art college. Except he had never finished the program.

It should have been a sign. Somehow, he had convinced a local hotel manager to take a chance on him and let him keep the books. He'd worked nights for a while, but never managed to make it through the probation period—some issue with a syringe someone found in the back stairwell.

Bill's idea of foreplay was cupping a breast and giving it three squeezes before climbing aboard. His raging stamina trumped his imagination, but it wasn't enough to keep the marriage viable.

'Newt's taking a long time in the shitter.' Liliana jiggles Bill's plate. 'Go check on him. He might have hurt himself.'

Bill's face turns crimson but he heads for the two-piece off the hallway, winding his way past Newt's paintings and Gerry's tin sculptures.

Liliana looks at Gerry and bursts out laughing. 'You look like a pirate,' she says.

'What are you on about now, woman?'

'There's a gob of newspaper dangling from your earlobe. Looks like an earring.'

'Says the person who steals from dumpsters!'

Aside from making sculptures, Gerry constructs mixed media collages of Liliana from wet newsprint and glue. When he works, the house reeks of an adhesive he makes himself out of corn syrup, water, cornstarch and vinegar. She finds sticky remnants everywhere—the windowsill, the kettle, the inside lip of the toaster. She doesn't love the images he makes—black and white, haunted looking, with shards of incomplete words littering her cheekbones. He's got her in corsets he creates from obituaries found in the newspaper. Her hair is a mess of paper ringlets. She doesn't wear fishnets in real life, yet he painstakingly crosshatches sexy hose on her make-believe legs. The installations leave her embarrassed yet at the same time yearning to be touched between the thighs.

Last month Gerry almost snagged a buyer for his work until

the collector stumbled upon a French Instagram artist whose work Gerry was clearly copying.

When Newt comes into the kitchen, Liliana pours him a cup of coffee and hands him a straw. The two had met as she was finishing up at a dumpster near where he was peddling his art. She melts as she gazes into his mocha-coloured eyes. He is the most handsome of the three artists, with wide cheekbones, a long, tapered nose and straight, white teeth.

She feels sorry that her ex-lover lost an entire arm and part of the other in an accident at the diner where he operated the dish sterilizer. But he made the best of his situation. He uses his feet to make art, gripping expired credit cards in his toes and smearing paint with wild abandon. He's on YouTube, and he makes money from the ads on his channel.

Liliana wipes her hands before slipping off her apron. The artists sit across from her, their mouths agape, waiting for her to dish up the fruit portion of their meal.

Newt manages to eat independently, his stump skating to the plate's rim where he hoovers food with waiting lips. Sometimes he uses his toes to hold chopsticks.

'Feeling better, Newt?' Liliana asks.

He'd always been her most considerate lover, the sort to put her needs first. What that man could do with his tongue! She misses that about him. A few days after the emergency amputation, his stump started emitting the pungent stench of rotting meat. Right away, she'd made sure to get him to the hospital to deal with what turned out to be a serious infection.

She watches with admiration as Newt bulldozes a huge piece of banana bread into his canyon mouth.

Gerry straightens and says, 'What you do with those clothes is a complete waste of time.'

'How's that, Ger?' Liliana says, her widened eyes unable to hide the resentment she felt brewing inside her.

'With your beautiful behind, you could make a fortune. You're sitting on a gold mine, girl!'

Bill guffaws and claps Gerry's shoulder. Liliana dumps a bowl of blueberries over Gerry's head.

'Aw, c'mon! Can't you take a joke?' Gerry wipes himself with his T-shirt. Smashed blueberries stain his head and face, the chunk of newsprint still swinging from his ear.

'Go fuck yourselves!' Liliana says.

Newt inhales what's left on his plate, snorting like a dog devouring kibbles from a bowl.

'A gold mine!' Gerry says.

Liliana stacks the dishes in the sink, cuts herself a wedge of banana bread, and heads to a downtown intersection that's busy with foot traffic, the location of her most fruitful donation bin. She's not there to drain the bin, though. She's there to observe the comings and goings of men who traverse the intersection, men who wear lined overcoats and perfectly tailored suits.

It doesn't cross Liliana's mind to seek love in a new locale. She is a woman shaped by pattern. The men she ogles are not artists; she's had it with them! These men wear silk neckties, dress shirts of varying hues. Their pants are pressed. She admires them for their dapperness and busy agendas. They are the sort to have certificates of completion on their walls, the sort to walk by and leave a whiff of aftershave trailing behind them.

One of the men is going bald. She has noticed him before. He's shorter than the other men, and there's something a bit lonely about the way his overcoat droops from his stooped shoulders. He wears it undone, too preoccupied to bother with the buttons. When a bus whips by, the coat momentarily flaps open, exposing a turquoise shirt she appraises as being in good taste and of fine quality.

Shortly after the traffic light changes, the man starts across the street towards her. His hands brush a steady rhythm against his thighs as he walks. When he gets closer, she notices that his fingernails appear recently manicured. He is obviously a man with a good-paying job, a desk job, someone who could look after her and treat her with respect.

She stands on the corner, willing their eyes to meet. She decides that, if he says hello, she will offer him a slice of the best banana bread in the whole wide world.

DONOR #0378Q

Blog Entry, evening of January 1
Currently: 183 lbs
Give up French fries for the foreseeable future

Like me, you have probably made a New Year's resolution or two. I have decided to give up something and add something. If I'm perfectly honest, I need to give up about ten things but how do-able is that? French fries, as stated above, is what I've decided to give up. Seriously, I love them but they aren't doing a single thing to help me fit into my jeans, even though I've taken to wearing elastic-waist ones.

Starting today, I'm keeping a food journal. It's nothing too fancy, just a calendar where I record what I eat and drink. I learned about it through one of my loyal blog followers who attends WW meetings. I'm tickled that I saved the WW fee, too.

Let me know in the comments below how your goals are coming along and if you need any encouragement.

* * *

Blog Entry, January 7
Currently: 182.5 lbs
Keeping a food journal has its benefits

Today's a bit of a bummer. It's the birthday of my deceased grandmother. She would have been 82. She and I shared a bedroom while I was growing up. We had a complicated relationship in my younger years, but after my father, her son, died, she mellowed. Didn't talk as loudly. Didn't complain as much about my clothes thrown on the floor. She started asking me to go out to coffee with her. Or, she'd ask to tag along when I went to the mall to window shop. We'd have nice talks about what it was like for her back in Europe around the time the Second World War broke out, about rations and selling stockings on the black market.

My daughter said I should make a cake for Great-Oma so I did. When I asked my daughter to help, she said she was too busy. I made carrot cake but skipped making the fancy cream cheese icing. After we blew out the candles, my daughter said the only good thing about carrot cake is the icing and next time not to bother if I'm not willing to frost it. She knows I'm trying to fit back into my clothes. I know she's only a kid, but I expected more compassion from her.

I dropped half a pound. How about you? Let me know in the comments below.

* * *

Blog Entry, January 18
Currently: 179 lbs
Joined a gym

My doctor suggested I start spin classes. The instructor had obviously been a teenager in the eighties. She plays Guns N' Roses, R.E.M., and Huey Lewis and the News. That and her constant yelling grate on my nerves. It's everything I can do to not plug my ears, but have you ever tried that while standing up on pedals of a bike, climbing an imaginary hill?

While I'm at spin class, I send my daughter to my mother's. I've heard all about how they bake cookies and eat sweets. I wish my mother would keep healthier options on hand, but of course she spoils my daughter. That's what grandmas do.

Let me know in the comments if you need help hitting your weight loss goals.

* * *

Blog Entry, February 8
Currently: 173 lbs
Ten pounds, bitches!

Did it! I achieved my initial weight loss goal. I don't mean to brag but I actually had to go out and buy some new clothes. Not too many, though, because I'm hoping to hit my next target by the end of March.

Spin class has turned out to be completely amazing. The instructor asked for feedback and boy, I wasn't the only one to shower her with criticism. Oh, I gave some tangible ideas, too. I suggested she use hand signals to tell us when to 'give it' and when to 'slow down'. Now I wear foam plugs in my ears so I get a break from her yelling and that horrid music.

I asked my daughter if she noticed mommy's weight loss. She said I always looked pretty to her, then sweetly asked for an ice cream bar. I knew it would ruin her dinner, but I couldn't help but give her one. She made a huge to-do of tearing off the wrapper as slowly as possible, and then ate it right in front of me. Used her bottom teeth to chip off the chocolate coating bit by bit. I had to leave the room to stop my cravings. But she hopped off her stool and followed me.

Let me know in the comments section if you'd cave if you were in my shoes.

* * *

Blog Entry, February 14
Currently: 175 lbs
Valentine's Day sucks

I don't know what happened. I was doing so well. My daughter
says she knows I cheat. That the only person I can blame is me.
That she hears me from her bedroom rooting around in the
kitchen for snacks. She even fished out of the garbage the wax
wrapper from the saltines I devoured. She left it in front of the
coffee machine so I'd know that she knew that I've been cheating
my diet.

I don't know about you, but I really detest, with a capital D,
Valentine's Day. I was tempted to make a reservation for me and
my daughter at a fancy-ass restaurant, but we've been on the
outs for a while now. I can't seem to get her under control. I
saw a poster on the bulletin board at the Independent Grocers
for parent education classes. But seriously, it's not *that* bad. Not
yet, anyway! I set up a swear jar, but she told me that's stupid.
That she doesn't have money so how can she contribute to the
swear jar? She's got a point. How many eight-year-olds do you
know who drop the f-bomb on a regular basis?

Anyway, looking forward to hearing your thoughts. I need
some parenting validation, folks. It's a lonely world for us Single
Moms by Choice.

* * *

Blog Entry, March 18
Currently: Who the hell knows? My scale broke.
Back on cigarettes (after reading about a teenager's premature
death from vaping)

If you are expecting a blog about weight loss goals today, I suggest
you come back another day. To be frank, I'm still reeling from

what happened. In fact, I don't have much energy to write today's post but you, my loyal followers, deserve to know what's going on.

It wasn't as though my daughter's sperm bank had been front and centre in my mind. Last week, when I opened the front door, I was handed a registered letter. I wasn't prepared for what came next. Three short paragraphs on Baby First Sperm Bank letterhead, signed by the manager of customer relations.

Paragraph two in particular left my legs wobbly. 'It is with great dismay that Baby First Sperm Bank must inform you of recently acquired information regarding your child's donor. Donor #0378Q just disclosed that he has, and has always had, a serious medical disorder that may impact the health of your child.'

I selected Baby First Sperm Bank for their rigorous screening procedures for HIV, Hepatitis B and C, and cystic fibrosis. But somehow, they'd failed to mention that the donor who seeded 73 live births was ill?

Seven years. That's how long I tried to conceive the conventional way. Three partners, all unwilling or unable to commit. I just wanted a baby. Was that too much to ask? So, I ended up approaching a guy at work.

Phil already had kids so I was confident his sperm were strong. He was married, but he swore he and his wife were throwing in the towel. He agreed to be a fully involved donor, maybe even a friend with benefits. But when his wife won that all-expenses-paid trip to Hawaii, their marriage issues vanished.

So, no baby with Phil.

What choice did I have? To the sperm bank I went.

Baby First's online sorting tool made it relatively easy to sift through the donors' details: ethnicity, age, height, and weight. Hair and eye colour. Overall health and emotional status. Hobbies and interests. Even whether the donor was into dogs or cats.

The profile I finally settled on was a Ukrainian-Canadian with thick blond hair.

I was in awe of the science and the possibilities. And my mother! A first-time granny at 58; I could barely scrape her off the ceiling.

Of course, there were issues. So much bloating. Headaches. Aches and pains. And injections to stimulate my ovaries. Genetic counselling, tests, poking and prodding. They'd turned me into a human pincushion. And the cost! But it was all going to be worth it.

How I fretted about my eggs and the donated seed in a Petri dish.

Implant day. Flat on my back on a gurney, my heels straining against cold metal stirrups. Faint images flickering from a monitor. The doctor tapping a screen, saying embryo this and embryo that. And then, just like that, a miracle was planted inside me.

The doctor said with a smile, *Now, don't forget to cross your legs.*

Fast forward to the second ultrasound, my bladder filled to the max. Granny-to-be's fingers digging into my arm with the tenacity of a toddler.

It's a she, said the doctor. *You're having a girl.*

If only the profile had made mention of the donor's medical issues. Did they really expect me to believe they had not known the donor's complete medical history prior to sending me the registered letter?

My daughter is short for her age. Barely three foot ten. She needs a stool to see herself in the bathroom mirror. Her eyes are the colour of coconuts, bottomless, callous. To look into them is to fall into the devil's breakfast. Her hair, dirty blond, thick and matted, looks as if she's just crawled out of bed.

I love her. I really do. But, mind you, she's a handful. It's more than the swearing. Last weekend, I found her over the toilet purging her supper. As difficult as it is to admit it, I lost it on her. I dragged her out of the bathroom and sat her down in the living room. I couldn't stop barraging her with questions. Why did she think she needed to do this? Who in the world had taught her how to throw up food? Was it someone at school? When did she start? Once I finally calmed down, I showered her with reassurances. Told her that she looked absolutely fine, that she was perfect just the way she was.

Know what she said was the reason? She wanted to make room for dessert.

To be honest, the donor's disclosure came as a strange kind of relief. I always suspected that my daughter's defiant attitude and uncontrollable appetite had a reasonable explanation. It's her sperm donor's fault—I'm sure of it. And to think that I almost blamed myself for failing as a mother! I know I'm sometimes too lenient. But I'm busy at the office all the time, and a consistent approach to parenting is just so much blessed work. I kept her in bed with me until she was six, even though experts, people who likely don't even have kids, say co-sleeping is a big no-no. But come on, we needed each other so much.

But now I can't help but wonder—were there other things in the donor's profile that I'd overlooked, that should have tipped me off? If there was something there that I'd missed, I'll never forgive myself. To think I'd read the dossier with such care!

Baby First has requested that I sign the enclosed form acknowledging receipt of the information about the donor. After that, they'll get consent from the donor to send a more detailed report about his history. Honestly, I don't know what to do.

What do you, my loyal followers, advise? I can't afford to pay much, but I hope one of you reading this blog is a lawyer who might have some insights to share. If the sperm donor made my baby ill, I'll sue him—and Baby First—and take them for every penny they have.

WET NURSE

On Friday nights Beth looked forward to hanging out with the Vixens for a night of wine and cards or a board game. The last Friday of the month was reserved for Truth or Dare, something the organizer of the group, Katelyn, had come up with. As the owner of a graphic art firm, Katelyn had the skills to create the question cards for the game.

During a recent Truth or Dare night, Beth drew Truth. She hardly ever pulled Truth, but when she did, she coped by coming up with something on the spot, some elaborate tall tale to titillate the Vixens while leaving her dignity intact. But not this time. This particular Friday night, possibly due to the third glass of Merlot she'd had, not her usual two, truth sat on her tongue and dared her to share.

On the night in question, Beth revealed a dark secret she'd managed to hold close to her chest for years: that she'd breastfed her infant nephew, Timmy.

The Vixens, most of them childless, gawked wide-eyed, salivating like hungry dogs wanting to get to the meat of what Beth had done. How it felt to feel Timmy on her nipple. How connected she and Timmy had become. Were they more than just auntie and nephew? Something closer, she thought, something akin to what she surmised twins might feel like. The more details she revealed, the dirtier they made her feel, what with their sniggering and condescending remarks. After a while their sneers made her feel so ashamed, she beat a hasty retreat just as an oversized metal platter of spring rolls was pulled from the bake oven.

She spent the rest of that Friday night at home, curled up on the floor in a fetal position, a hand tucked between her legs.

In the following weeks, Beth tried to glue the pieces of her self-respect back together. If only she could forgive herself for her stupidity; spilling the truth to the Vixens had obviously been a serious mistake. She should have known. They were an uptight bunch, despite their collective desire to be forward-thinking and hip. Rapinder, a librarian of environmental sciences at the university, couldn't utter the word 'orgasm' for fear of causing a week of bad karma. Katelyn could, but only because she'd faked so many in the past.

Beth didn't owe them a single thing. The group was comprised of mealy-mouthed women who'd happened to meet and connect at a Paint Night at the community centre a couple of years back. It was Katelyn Beth felt she had to watch out for. Katelyn loved nothing more than wielding her coercive energy whenever the Vixens got together.

Beth couldn't see herself returning to the Vixens, so she started skipping Friday night cards and end-of-month Truth or Dare. She manufactured excuses: a toothache, a stomach virus, a mysterious rash. Texts queued up on her smartphone pleading to know where she was and why she wasn't coming. So, she deleted them. First the texts, then the contacts.

* * *

Since Beth was often short on time, she usually shopped at Kim's, the neighbourhood market. No wax-polished produce there, no jumbo-sized shopping carts nudging a person to overspend. One morning she walked three blocks to the store, her collapsible metal cart clanging along behind her. Beth paused to catch her breath when she heard a familiar voice.

'Beth? You shop here?' It was Katelyn, the one who had brought the Vixens together and who had come up with the name for the group in the first place.

'You startled me,' Beth said.

Beth took in Katelyn's crimson stockings and short black dress with off-white lace circling the neckline—quite a get-up for grocery shopping. Beth adjusted her oversized T-shirt to cover her stained shorts. 'I live just around the corner now. I couldn't afford my old place after my apartment-mate moved out.'

'I remember you mentioning that. Of course, I'm on Stanley,' Katelyn said, her head nodding like one of those plastic dogs in the back of a station wagon. 'We've missed you on Fridays, especially at Truth or Dare,' she said with a wink.

'Um, I've been putting in a lot of overtime. Our firm just secured a large engineering contract with the city.' Beth's eyes darted around in search of an escape.

'I texted but—'

'Yeah, like I said—'

'We all lead hectic lives. Getting together on Friday nights is how we sisters blow off steam.'

This thing with Katelyn felt like a cross-examination. It wasn't like Beth owed Katelyn or the rest of them anything. Since she'd stopped going, she'd felt pleased with herself to be reading from a stack of novels at the back of her closet.

'So, we'll see you at Rapinder's at the end of the month?'

'I'm—'

'What's that?'

'It's just—'

'You're embarrassed? Humiliated? Of course, who wouldn't be? But it's not exactly the end of the world, now, is it? The whole nephew thing was a shocker, but you have to admit, it was also pretty funny. The look on Rapinder's face was priceless,' Katelyn said, resting a hand on Beth's arm. 'Promise to come.'

'I'll—'

'Think about it.'

And as quickly as Katelyn appeared, she vanished.

It had been a couple of months since the big reveal. Beth wasn't sure if she should hang out with middle-aged women whose claim to fame was a shared disappointment in men, a disappointment sometimes verging on loathing. But then again, Beth didn't want to be hasty. She would have to see how she felt as the end of the month crept closer. She had to admit; she missed playing canasta and Monopoly on Fridays. But was she ready to resume Truth or Dare?

The exchange with Katelyn left her feeling weak, wrung out. She barely had the strength to check the flyers, but for once, no one was standing in front of the bulletin board Mr Kim kept next to the briquettes and bottle return.

DOG-WALKER.

TROUBLE WITH YOUR TAXES?

SPARE ROOM FOR LEASE

WET NURSE REQUIRED/CERTIFIED TEMP AGENCY

Because someone had tucked the wet nurse ad behind one about an allergy study, Beth almost missed it. She had left her reading glasses next to the coffee maker at home so she had to squint to see the details.

There were things Beth had not told the Vixens, let alone revealed to her real sister: sacred truths, like the buzz Timmy's lips provided on her engorged nipple. She liked his little tongue a lot, maybe too much. When Beth closed her eyes and synced herself to the rhythm of his suckling, she felt something in the way he used his mouth which no boyfriend had ever been able to match.

Wet nurse. Hell, why not?

If the temp agency selected her, she was sure she'd have no problem convincing them that she was a good fit. Her sister, surely, would provide a stellar reference. Beth prided herself on eating healthy, avoiding drugs, and walking ten thousand steps a day. She wasn't averse to ingesting new foods, or homeopathic tinctures with obscure names like fenugreek and blessed thistle. Anything to promote lactation.

With the contact information for the temp agency tucked safely inside her handbag, Beth made her way home.

There were times when Beth felt that nursing Timmy may have built a wall between her and her sister. Maybe it was perceived jealousy. Beth often wondered how her sister could stand to watch Beth breastfeed her son. After the arrangement was over, for a while Beth's sister only texted once in a while, mostly when she or Timmy needed something. Beth tried not to be overly sensitive. People, especially those with children, became consumed with the everyday busyness of life.

Beth took her time putting away the groceries before heading for the bathroom. Standing in front of the mirror, she pulled her T-shirt over her head and admired her perfectly symmetrical breasts. Not too large, not too small. Prominent nipples on areolas the size of clementines. Because years before she'd been fitted for a support bra, they hadn't sagged a bit.

With a dab of lotion on each forefinger, she drew circles around her nipples, each movement bringing her milk closer to finding its way. She knew exactly what to look for. When the time was right, her hands cupped her breasts. She closed her eyes for this part and gave each nipple a subtle pinch and there it was. She felt it, that tiny burst, a letting go of sorts, the teeniest of droplets, like a gentle spritz from an aerosol can. If the temp agency asked, she'd assure them that she could do it on demand, as she had before. Without ever having given birth.

* * *

Friday night is a cheerless time for lonely women, especially when their co-workers wish them a terrific weekend and then go off to their partners and kids, or on a date. That is why, minutes before quitting time, Beth decided to head to Rapinder's. Rather than wasting time going home to eat and get a change of clothes, she grabbed a bite at the food truck outside the office.

In the rideshare, Beth detected a rank smell and silently blamed the driver. She cringed when she realized it was her. She begged the driver to stop and wait at a drugstore while she bought a bottle of body spray, so she was an hour late by the time she arrived at her friend's place. When she stepped off the elevator, raucous laughter told her the Vixens had been hitting the Merlot.

A handmade banner dangled from the kitchen cupboards: B O O B S. Sheila, an elementary school special education teacher, was softly swaying on her seat as if a love song were playing in her head, despite the lively version of the game that was underway. Rapinder, too, rocked back and forth to beats coursing through her veins. The poster and temperature of the room caused Beth to pause and reconsider her decision to take part. The night had the possibility of becoming quite a ride. Yet, to Beth, the first few questions she listened to seemed innocuous, non-threatening, and humdrum.

When did your boobs begin to sag?

Do you ever go braless?

Is one boob bigger? Prove it for extra points.

Which would you rather? Give up your boobs or gain a hundred pounds?

It was Sheila's turn. Beth checked out Sheila's prepubescent-looking chest and sighed. Big boobs would overpower her child-sized frame.

Do you ever touch yourself?

Have you ever gone topless in public?

What is your favourite erogenous zone?

All sorts of questions. Nothing Beth couldn't handle.

* * *

When Katelyn returned from the bathroom, her sweat-dampened bangs were clumped against her forehead, something that only happened when she drank hard and fast.

Katelyn, her voice louder than necessary, said, 'You're finally here, Bethie! Just in time for another couple of rounds.'

'Of wine?' Sheila asked.

'The game, you twit,' Katelyn said, touching up her lips without benefit of a mirror.

Beth drew the top card from the deck of Katelyn's homemade but professional-looking cards. Truth.

'Be honest. When was the last time you had sex?'

'Easy. Can't remember.'

'Sounds about right. Likely been so long your hymen's grown back,' someone called out.

Another truth card. 'What word best describes your social life?'

'Ah, like yours. Pretty much non-existent.'

The room filled with nervous giggles.

Another card. Truth again.

Sheila began to read but Katelyn snatched the card from her. Her eyes zeroed in on Beth's before she read the card. 'Describe that time your nipple found its way into the mouth of a babe not your own.'

'This again?' Beth asked.

'You owe us,' Katelyn said, sliding a mini-carrot between her teeth.

She had to refrain from rolling her eyes at these women, these voyeurs who aroused themselves by asking stupid questions about each other's sex lives. She didn't owe them anything. She knew what they were—divorced, never married, unhappily married, one of them a single mom, all of them as frustrated as she. And yet, in the days leading up to Truth or Dare night, Beth had felt a compulsion to show up, to speak her mind.

'Trust us,' Katelyn said, her crooked smile bursting from a sea of freckles.

Beth remained silent. She didn't trust them one bit.

Katelyn said, louder than the small living room required, 'You spilling the beans or not? Answer truthfully or forfeit your points.'

'Okay, okay. But, to be clear, things didn't unfold like you think.'

Beth slipped an elastic band from her wrist and tied her hair back.

'I couldn't just pop a nipple into Timmy's mouth.' The smell of sausages sizzling under the broiler filled the apartment. 'I had to teach my breasts to do what breasts do best: make milk.'

As she said this, Beth slowly undid the buttons of her blouse. This was her moment. She'd held onto the secret so long, the power held deep inside her breasts. The time was ripe for her to divulge what she'd been concealing. But she wanted to make them wait a moment or two longer. To take it slowly. To make them beg for it. The room fell silent as she undid the clasp on her bra; mouths fell open as she kneaded her nipples. Beth had their full attention now.

Suddenly, the Vixens were green-eyed preteens gawking at the swelling breasts of a grown woman. When Sheila leaned in for a closer look, she fell against the coffee table, her glass of wine spilling onto the cheese tray.

'Ah, shit,' Sheila said, jumping up for a tea towel.

'I felt like I was training for the breastfeeding Olympics,' Beth said while rubbing, pulling, and coaxing her nipples. 'My hands saying WAKE UP, MILK GLANDS.'

After taking the snack out of the oven, Rapinder threw herself against the sofa, and sighed. 'Wow. What a rush.'

'Pretty effing awesome, if you ask me,' someone said.

'Wait,' Beth said, 'There's more.

'It took a month or so because these things take time but my breasts jumped two sizes. Rounder, fuller, less tender, and then—and this is the amazing part—I could feel that my nipples were moist.'

'Wait a second. Don't you have to have had a baby to make milk?' a voice asked.

'In fact,' Beth said, 'you don't. That's a myth.'

'Explain yourself,' Sheila said.

'Breastfeeding without giving birth has been possible for years, but with the introduction of formula, it became less common. The only necessary component of lactation is to stimulate and train the breasts to produce and drain themselves of milk.'

It was Katelyn who spoke next. 'Why didn't your sister nurse her own damned kid?' The Vixens nodded their heads, wanting to know.

'A good question but first, I need fortification,' Beth said, holding out her glass. She looked around; she had them where she wanted them.

Rapinder said, 'There's only white left.'

'That's fine. The thing is, pregnancy made my sister develop aversions. Raw chicken. Ketchup chips. Litter boxes. Black liquorice. Onions sautéing in a pan. And breastfeeding. She couldn't stomach the idea of it.'

'Somebody else's kid sucking on me is something I wouldn't have the stomach for either!' Sheila said. 'I mean, how could you?'

'How could I? More like how could I not? She's my sister; he's my nephew.'

'I'm with Sheila. I couldn't do it,' Rapinder said, folding her arms across her chest.

'Rapinder,' said Katelyn, 'you'd have to have at least been with a man to know what we're talking about here.'

'I've been with—'

'Necking with your third-cousin doesn't count.'

Rapinder pushed from her seat, wobbled slightly, and said, 'That is bullshit! I have never ever done that.' She quickly sat down in a huff.

Beth said, 'Here's what you don't get. The idea of a tiny mouth on my sister's nipple made her queasy.'

'What about formula?'

'Yeah, or why couldn't your sister pump?'

'Her own kid's mouth sucking on her made her feel sick?' Katelyn said. 'Yet she expected you to do it? That's nuts, don't you think?'

'You'd have to know my sister, that's all,' Beth said, luxuriating in the excitement she'd created in the room.

'Oh, my God!' Katelyn said. 'This is all so weird.'

'Wait a second? What about her *husband*?' Sheila asked.

'What about him?'

'Surely to God your sister isn't … wasn't … repulsed by him, you know—'

'Touching her?' Beth shrugged. 'Well, that's different, don't you think? Or maybe that was part of her aversion, that Timmy's mouth might feel, well, sexual.' Beth wasn't sure how she could better describe her sister's exact hang-up. All Beth could glean was her sister believed that breastfeeding was sexual, and believing it messed with the intimacy between her and her husband.

Katelyn ran a moist finger along the top of her wine glass, causing it to shriek. 'You should have brought her tonight.'

'My sister?'

'Yeah. Why don't you next time?'

Beth looked around the room dubiously. 'Why? So, you could put her under the microscope?' Not bloody likely.

'I think she'd be interesting,' Katelyn said, heading into the kitchen for more wine. 'We could get the information straight from her.'

'I manually pumped so they could be involved in feeding the baby. Both of them helped,' Beth said.

'Her husband helped pump?' Rapinder said.

The group burst out laughing.

'I couldn't stand the mechanical pump. All that slurping noise. He was there mostly for support. To encourage me to keep going.'

Beth paused and looked around the room.

Sheila crossed and uncrossed her legs, then sat up straighter before saying, 'Didn't your sister object?'

Beth leaned back and chuckled. 'My sister knew breast was best.'

'Just not hers,' Katelyn added. She had just returned from the kitchen and her bangs were damper and clumpier than ever.

'Because my breasts were so willing, my sister didn't need much convincing. A few days before the due date, I moved into the room next to the nursery. Stayed with them for over a year.'

Beth stood up and walked over to the sliding door, which led out to Rapinder's balcony. Studying the reflection of her breasts in the glass, she said, 'It's hard to believe how fast the years slip by. Timmy's off to school in the fall.'

* * *

Overall, it had been a successful evening. The balance of power had shifted and, instead of Beth, it seemed likely Rapinder would become Katelyn's next target. Even better, the Vixens had been mesmerized by what Beth had shared. What she hadn't told the Vixens was how close she and her sister had become through the experience, so close they now lived in adjoining apartments.

In the elevator, Beth opened a text message from her sister.

If you have time after the Vixens, stop by. Timmy can't fall asleep without a cuddle from his Auntie Beth.

Beth texted back: *I'll be right over.*

SOMETHING FOR RAIN

Dear Rain,

Last night I was thinking about when we were little kids. We were looking forward to going to the fall fair. It had poured buckets all week and the fair almost got canned. You were seven, and I had just begun grade six. They'd spread straw around the midway to soak up the puddles. We each gripped a roll of quarters. Your tube was so tight your fingertips turned cherry red trying to bust out the coins. But we got you fixed up. You played a balloon-popping game until your arm wore out. I still have that felt porpoise you won. I never expected the carnival guy to fix it so a little kid like you could win.

I don't have a brilliant excuse for not writing except that things have been hectic. And because I haven't written in a while, I've got tons of news. Sorry to hear your prime worker is leaving. I liked that girl but can't for the life of me remember her name. She always offered a sparkling smile and intriguing stories about that uncle of hers who works in the tunnels under the falls.

I can't eat lemon squares anymore. You know the ones? Dick used to bring them home from East Side Mario's. Dick said they're made in a factory in Brantford. That just spoiled it for me. I preferred thinking Dick's team baked them on site. Fresher that way instead of hours getting jostled in the back of a trailer. I hate eating things out of a box. Anyway, whenever I have them now, my lips break out in a rash.

Dick's promotion from line cook to chef happened faster

than any of us guessed. Mom says it's because he has a culinary diploma from George Brown, but I suspect it's something else. I've caught myself looking at him more like a guy than a stepdad. When he pours milk into a glass, blond hairs glisten on the muscles of his arms.

A few months back, Dick bought me a Barbie. I reminded him I was turning fifteen. He clicked his tongue on his teeth and said, 'One day you're a little girl chewing the feet off your dollies and then, snap, it's over.'

I have a feeling Mom kept it from you about the cat. You know how Alex always had that habit of over-grooming? Dick was sprawled in that blue lounger he brought over when he and Mom moved in together. He was sucking back a beer and pressing buttons on the remote trying to track down a ball game. I was at work at the roller-skating place.

Mom said Alex's mistake was sauntering into the TV room. He took a huge yawn with his tail up and his front paws in a downward dog, aimed his butt right at Dick's lounger, and sprayed. Dick lost it. He smacked Alex right into the TV console. Mom made Dick take him for an X-ray. Busted pelvis. Dick said, 'No way I'm paying for surgery on a stray.' So he had him put down. I'm sorry you weren't home to say goodbye. If I concentrate, I can still feel Alex's sandpaper tongue.

I have a pile of homework so I've got to go for now. I love you, buddy. I'll write again soon. I promise.

Storm

* * *

Dear Rain,

I have news. I moved out. I'm in a special home not unlike yours at Linkletter. Mine is for girls having a baby. I moved in two months ago. Mom wouldn't even let me borrow a suitcase. Something about her and Dick maybe flying south. So I packed everything in a garbage bag like I was donating to the Sally Ann. Anyway, I'm here until the baby comes, which should be in a few months.

You remember that boy I told you I was going out with? We broke up. I know. You must be surprised. It was shortly after Mom caught us. Mom and Dick were heading over to a dance so me and Meyer decided to take our time, you know, messing around. It was my idea to do it in their bed. They drove all the way to the dance and changed their minds. I think they had an argument or something. Mom came into the house yodeling like she does. Me and Meyer's legs were tangled in their sheets. We never heard a thing.

Then, all of a sudden, Mom was holding the bedroom door open and the hallway light was like a blinding halo around her head. 'In our bed?' she yelled. 'You're doing it *in our bed*?'

She was so angry she ripped off the sheets. I did everything I could to cover my girl parts. It's been years since Mom's seen me naked. Meyer was skipping around, looking for something to throw over his shrivelled bits. Then Mom screamed, 'Get out before Dick finds you and kicks your sorry asses.'

Anyway, when I walked Meyer home, we scrapped like crazy. At first it was about getting caught by Mom. That whole scene was beyond humiliating. But then we ended up fighting because I caught wind that Meyer had been seen hanging around downtown with a girl, Cassidy, who I thought was my bestie. I told him I obviously couldn't trust him anymore so we ended up splitting after that. Mom and Dick certainly screwed things up coming home so early.

When you were in grade four you had that teacher, Mrs Wilson, who was pregnant with twins. She got huge as a water boiler. Her belly button poked out of her blouse and was as round as a kiwi. Mine popped at five months. I have to put tape on it to smooth it out. My skin crawls with prickly itch. I like using the bamboo scratcher Mom brought home from Phoenix. I scrape until there's red splotches from my boobs to my privates. I scratch until I can't take it anymore and then I slather myself in Gold Bond Anti-itch Cream.

Speaking of boobs, mine are enormous. Three sizes up. My breasts look like cats in sacks. They're lumpy and streaked in ugly blue lines. You know how pale my skin usually is, especially in winter. The nipples are dark and nasty and they're as big as cup saucers. Maybe this isn't something for me to be telling my brother. Sorry for grossing you out.

My room is for girls giving up their babies. No parenting moms live in this part of the facility. This one girl named Angel is having her second baby. She lives in a room around the corner and three doors up from mine. Children's Aid took her first baby because she and the daddy were using drugs. After an ultrasound, the doctor said this second baby isn't developing properly and Angel still won't agree to terminate. She says it doesn't matter what she decides because it'll get taken from her anyway.

I have to get ready for dinner in the dining hall. I'm on kitchen cleanup tonight.

Love you.

Storm

* * *

Dear Rain,

It's been pouring here off and on for over two weeks. At least when the air is moist I don't chafe as much. A girl down the hall recommended bathing in oatmeal. I tried it a couple times but felt queasy after. It's likely from reaching into the corners of the tub to scrape the oats down the drain.

Before I moved out, a social worker from Linkletter was over for a meeting with the family. Both Mom and Dick got all dressed up. Mom wore a black skirt and a white blouse with a little bit of lace edging the collar. Dick wore the outfit he usually wears for church, and he even put on cufflinks. Mom fussed around making coffee and tea, and Dick brought home lemon squares from the restaurant.

The social worker recommended Mom and Dick have more visits with you. She showed them a summary of their annual visits taken from the facility records. She said, 'The last time you were there was over six months ago.' She pointed at a graph. 'And you only stayed fifteen minutes. This won't help Rain develop to his potential.'

Because no questions were asked, Mom didn't say anything. She kept pushing coffee and tea. She stirred three lumps of sugar into her cup and the metal spoon sounded like steel drums against the porcelain. From my spot behind their bedroom door, it was evident Dick was waiting for the meeting to end. He fumbled open a pack of playing cards and started lining the cards up for a game of Solitaire.

'And Storm? I hear she's still writing to Rain. That's good. She could go and visit, too. Is she here today?' asked the worker.

Dick waved a hand at no one in particular and said, 'Storm's a good girl. This here, though, this is a meeting for adults, not her. Let's leave her out of it.'

I could see the worker's back stiffen. Then she repeated her comment about them never visiting. Rather than feeling disappointed in himself, Dick held his shoulders back and rested a lemon square between his lips while Mom stared at her coffee.

The worker said, 'Rain's placement may be in jeopardy if you don't become more involved.'

Dick said, 'You think you've got all the angles covered, eh?' He slid his chair over so he was closer to the worker. He rubbed his hands together as if doing so would make the woman disappear. 'It isn't likely to make any difference. Rain's not all there,' he said, tapping his head.

Mom excused herself to go to the bathroom. I could hear her wailing over the water running into the basin. Dick stood up and spoke to the worker so softly I couldn't make it out. I figured it wasn't anything good on account of the worker's face flushing crimson before she tossed all her charts and graphs into her briefcase and took off.

When I missed my first period, I freaked. I thought my uterus must be riddled with tumours and that a doctor would have to dig them out. I knew me and Meyer hadn't actually done it. Sure, we'd messed around and he'd rubbed up and down between my legs but I knew I couldn't get pregnant from that. So I did what any pregnant kid did when she didn't want anyone to know. I half-starved myself to keep from gaining weight. But Mom eventually pieced it together, and she slapped the backs of my legs with a fly swatter she was so pissed. Turns out she'd been keeping a tally on how many sanitary pads were left in the box.

When me and Meyer broke up, Mom hinted maybe it was because Meyer couldn't handle the pregnancy. She doesn't know him like I do. He's great with kids. She said, 'You have to tell Meyer. He has a right.'

Of course, I said I'd already told him. Only I never did.

There's a school here. Just like you have at Linkletter. It's cool. We have two teachers. I wear pyjamas and slippers to class because the classroom is down the hall from the residence. We work out of independent study booklets. I like learning this way. I don't have to read out loud like I would in a normal school. I study English from 9:00 until lunch. I'll wait and do math after the baby's born.

My room smells slightly musty, like old sneakers or ice skates. The staff person tells me it's because the room is sometimes used to store donations of gently used clothes from the community. I have places to put stuff. There's a night table with drawers where I keep my journal, a pen, and my makeup. When I first moved in, there were three cribs stored in my room, but someone took them out while I was getting registered. The walls are painted a light shade of grey. There's a little TV on a desk. It only gets one channel and usually I just watch game shows. There aren't enough hangers so I pile my clothes on a chair. There's a red and black quilt on the single bed. It reminds me of the one that used to be on your bed. I wish I could thank the volunteers who stitched it.

I brought my keepsake box. I still have that photograph of you from Sunfish Lake, taken just before you nearly drowned. I snitched some hairs from your baby book and taped them to the back of the picture. Dad's in that photo. And Mom. I think about Dad a lot, especially now with what's going on. I can still see him—how he paddled so hard rescuing you but didn't save a breath for himself. Dad's body just floating there a few feet from the beach. Mom wringing her hands.

I have a photo of my baby. It's called a sonogram, and it's a computerized picture the ultrasound technician prints off. You'll be happy to know that so far the baby is perfect. When the doctor told me the sex, he said, 'Your baby comes with a handle,' which means I'm having a boy.

There are a couple other things in the box. There's that ball of yellow yarn we used to throw at Alex. Remember that time he spun out of control and shredded Mom's good curtains? Boy, did she get pissy. Dick promised to buy her a new set and he did. They are rose-coloured and kind of clash with the gold sofa and his blue lounge chair. But Mom says it was a kind gesture. The last thing in the box is an index card with the name and address of Mom's friend in Guelph. That's where I'm aiming to go after I leave here.

Love you always,
Storm

* * *

Dear Rain,

It's been decided. The baby is going to a home with two dads. I interviewed a million people. So many nice couples dying for a newborn. It became a toss-up between Rahim and Darwinder and Stan and Peter. Rahim and Darwinder were quite suitable, but because Stan and Peter are guys who can never, ever make their own kid, I ended up picking them.

You should have seen the work that went into the videos and photo albums those guys made. Peter is the creative one. For each page he used a different blue background. One page showed the kind of books they already bought to read to the baby. Another one featured their home, which is more castle than house. The music they picked for the video was 'Endless Love'. Anyway, it was a tough decision, but I am sticking with it. The best part is I didn't have to tell Rahim and Darwinder. My social worker did that for me.

You'd like Stan. He's a preschool teacher. He's super tall, lanky, just turned thirty-one, with spiky hair and John Lennon glasses. He has a hint of whiskers. When he was still in his twenties, he competed in cross-country ski racing for Canada. I googled his name to find out more.

Peter is a sculpture artist. He's kind of stout, with medium brown hair greying at the temples. His face is round with a reddish complexion, like Dick's gets when he drinks. Peter has sculpted three prime ministers, and they're on display in a big city I can't remember the name of.

They both want me to stay involved with the baby. I don't really get the details of this three-parent set-up, but I told my social worker I'd consider it.

I was in the dining room when a page came over the PA. It was just as one of the mom's babies started puking and everyone was saying things like, 'Gross' and 'Do something!'

The social worker was calling to inquire about my decision

on co-parenting. I took the phone call at the front desk, away from the drama. When the social worker asked me if I wanted to stay involved, I was admittedly conflicted. Part of me wanted to. So when she asked again, the words got stuck in my throat and I just couldn't say them. So when the social worker said all the right things, explaining the benefits to everyone involved, all I had to say was, 'All right.'

Because my baby isn't born yet, to fill the day between classes, I volunteer in the kitchen. I'm glad I don't have to take the parenting courses. That would suck. I help Cook Mara peel carrots for stew or chop up cabbage for soup. She's quite grumpy. Last week she caught me with unwashed hands as I was grabbing a potato peeler. She marched me into the dining room and said, 'Storm is now on a week's probation for having dirty hands in the kitchen.' I heard a gasp from a couple girls who think they are cooler than everyone. I felt terrible until I remembered you pulling boogers from your nose and then eating them.

I have to go do some laundry. I'll visit as soon as I squeeze this baby out.

Storm

* * *

Hey Rain,

A few nights ago, a mom who gave twins up for adoption returned from hospital to the residence. After convalescing here, she'll be getting an apartment. Her milk just came in and a staff member bound her breasts with a strip of bedding. The girl cried herself to sleep, and in the morning I stopped by her room to check in. She showed me where her boobs leaked all over the mattress. Her room smells like canned pears gone bad.

Mom asked to be with me for the delivery. I don't have anyone else arranged and I'm supposed to have a coach there. I obviously can't ask the baby's daddy.

When Mom got offered the early morning bakery shift eight months ago, she said, 'It pays an extra seventy-five cents an hour.'

'Then you should do it,' Dick said.

A few days after Mom started the shift, Dick looked over at me with his head tilted upward and then looked at the ceiling like he was questioning a higher authority. From his pocket, he withdrew a five-dollar bill, which he squeezed into my hand.

'For a hug sometime,' he said.

And I don't know why but I said, 'Thank you. I'd like that.'

If you were me right now, what would you do? I feel sticky and dirty but, when I take a shower and wash my clothes, I feel clean. I notice my cheeks have a new dimple. It makes me think I've found a kind of happiness. I own my own smile.

Love you, Rain.

Storm

BREAK TIME

The sky is mulberry when Ambrosia pulls into the employee parking lot of The Ontario Envelope Company—TOE as it is known in the valley. She walks toward the factory, popping a handful of salted almonds into her mouth, mashing them into a pulp, then tucking the wad against her cheek. She stops at the change room and opens her locker. After fussing with her hair, she tugs on the regulation uniform: yellow jumpsuit and matching booties, bonnet, and mask. She leaves the gloves for later. En route to custodial services, she lets her eyes linger on the steel-blue polish of her fingernails.

She likes picking up extra shifts for the money and for the time away from home. She's thinking about saving up for a dog—not just any kind of dog, but an Alaskan Klee Kai, a husky miniaturized to grow no taller than seventeen inches. A forever puppy, something she could love and cuddle like she'd always wanted since she was little. But Tom claims he's allergic.

She pours detergent into her mop bucket and as it swirls, an image of her boyfriend pops into mind: his fat ass on her sofa, a video game controller in hand, empty beer cans strewn here and there. Ambrosia is increasingly convinced she would prefer a puppy's occasional messes on the carpet to the debris that orbits Tom in the living room.

Things have soured between them so much that she and Tom have almost completely stopped talking. When he asks her something, she always seems to be in another room and cannot hear him. When she has no choice but to speak to him, she keeps her answers to *yes* or *no*.

Tom doesn't like that Ambrosia has rediscovered her passion for astrology. In the beginning, she'd tried bringing up his sign as a means of better understanding him. 'You Virgos are all the same,' she had said the other day, pulling up his birth chart on her phone.

'Not this again,' he said, his lips curling. 'I've told you a million times. That stuff is bullshit!'

'It's not. Just hear me out. Everyone knows that Virgos—'

He picked up the controller and returned to his game. She stared at his once slim build, now bloated and flabby. His dark hair, which he used to keep neatly trimmed, was now long and unkempt, pulled into a ponytail and fastened with a twist tie. She remembered with wistful desire the lean body and sinewy muscles of his roofing days.

Their first date had been a casual meet-up on the patio of a local café. Both had ordered lattes in paper cups, his with sugar, hers without. Hers came without a paper sleeve. When she complained that the cup was too hot, he made a huge show of wrestling the paper sleeve from his cup and slipping it onto hers. It was then that he told her he was a Virgo—such a practical sign, she thought.

He had been in first year computer science, and she told him she was between courses. Her days in community college had been brief. She'd been so easily distracted from studying. Dungeons and Dragons. Spoken word poetry. Astrology. Ping pong. Guitar lessons. The most interesting thing she had done in college was dig out a clump of non-indigenous plants from the garden in front of her residence. Her grades had been so low the dean had asked her to withdraw for a year and get her priorities straightened out.

Getting kicked out of school meant devoting herself full-time to Tom. She had filled her days and nights with 'Dating Tom', a term she affectionately coined for him. They'd already been going out for three months before they made love for the first time. She liked that he'd wanted to wait, as if playing hard-to-get would make her fall harder for him. He didn't wait long to propose, though. Within six months of meeting, he invited her to the beach where he'd placed rocks on the shore to spell out MARRY ME.

'Engaged Tom' was soft and kind. He rubbed her feet after she'd spent a long day on them. He offered to take out the trash when he noticed it was full. He hosed down her car when it was grimy from driving on gravel roads. Engaged Tom was a thought-ful, patient lover who took his time with foreplay, looking after her needs before seeing to his.

When she asked to meet his family, though, a red flag popped up. He would book a time for Ambrosia to meet them and then he'd cancel at the last minute, claiming to have been called into work or have trouble with his truck. When she asked him to rebook, he said he'd rather focus on the two of them, on building a happy future together, that they had all the time in the world for her to bond with his family. She didn't end up meeting his parents until a week prior to the wedding.

Engaged Tom pointed out that he didn't love when Ambrosia wore overalls on the weekends, that her choice of outfit reminded him of the carpenters at the worksite. That he pre-ferred her to wear form-fitting jeans, something more stylish and flattering. While dating he asked her opinion on what show to watch on Netflix but Engaged Tom didn't seem to care. He decided for them even when she insisted she wasn't in the mood for *CSI Las Vegas*. And he called her stupid when she didn't know what was going on in the plotline of *Killing Eve*. And it was curi-ous that none of Tom's friends had ever been over.

Despite these issues, she had looked the other way and

married him in a simple ceremony at city hall with their parents as witnesses.

It was shortly after the wedding that Tom went from enchanting to mildly irritating to tedious to obnoxious. At the bar he had a habit of worming into conversations and then getting upset when the people around him didn't laugh at what he had to say. He had even picked a few fights with guys—complete strangers—over minor things, like who was going to win the Stanley Cup that year. Her friends stopped accepting invitations to hang out. Tom's friends were never around, so they spent more and more time alone. Tom soon took Ambrosia for granted. When she cooked for him, he didn't say thank you or help put the dishes into the sink.

Now she can't even remember the last time she and Tom made love. Apathy and excuses had replaced desire.

Somehow, in all of this, Ambrosia had let her dreams fall to the wayside. After the fiasco of college, she'd intended to travel the world, become drunk on high altitudes, sink her toes into every ocean, sleep in train stations on each continent and collect sand from every seashore. She planned to store the sand in jars on her dresser to remind herself that she was capable of spontaneity and fun, of drinking the very marrow out of life.

Now her dream was as mundane as getting a dog.

At break time, Ambrosia twists off the lid on her thermos. The smell of butter chicken fills the air. She opens the window blinds to reveal the moon, a sickle against the solemn sky.

Tom falling off the roof and fracturing his back had done nothing but shine a spotlight on the cracks of their already failing marriage. More than once, she'd considered packing her bags and sneaking out while he was passed out from pain meds and beer. She'd probably have divorced him if the accident hadn't happened, but now he faced a permanently ruined back. She couldn't leave him under the circumstances. Tom had no one else, and she was keenly aware of how viciously people would judge her. On the other hand, she was losing patience with the way he was using his back injury as an excuse to play video games all day while tossing back beers and toking up. *Medical marijuana, my ass!* Ambrosia thinks.

She believes life is about sacrifices, but living with a parasite isn't the sort of sacrifice Ambrosia had in mind. She feels as if she is crawling along a gravel road, every bump and sharp stone digging into her palms and knees, a punishment for her good deeds. She wants to roll off the trail and seek adventure. Forage for sprouts, leaves, nuts, berries and roots that she can munch on or take home to simmer in a pot or add to a salad. She's wondered about geocaching, a hobby that involved visiting new places and using a navigation app to find treasures hidden behind boulders, in trees, or even under park benches in urban areas. Nothing was stopping her from going paragliding. Or learning orienteering.

She doesn't want to spend the next forty years mopping up after people.

But Tom is stopping her. Tom and his damned back pain.

The fall off the roof ruined the one thing in their marriage that had worked: Tom's ability to provide for her.

The doctor said, 'His back is broken. He may never walk again. Prepare yourself,' but Tom had surprised everyone. He had rallied. After three surgeries and months of physiotherapy, she had brought him home. But the guy who had once enjoyed a straight posture and fluid movements now hobbled to the toilet, stooped at the waist. For a while Ambrosia walked next to him, a steady hand on his elbow, to ensure he didn't pitch over and reinjure himself. The guilt of him further damaging himself was more than she could bear.

She wishes she could feel sorry for him. But she can't help thinking that it's his own fault that he'd become doughy around the neck and middle. His hygiene had taken an unnecessary turn for the worse. He claims the water pressure aggravates his already sore back, but she doesn't believe it. The only time he looks energetic is when Canada Post drops off his weed. When he opens the door he rubs his palms together and says the same lame thing: 'Get me my rolling papers, baby!'

The day Tom tumbled off the roof, the foreman had called her at work. 'There's been a terrible accident. Your husband has been taken to Mary Magdalene Hospital. Please come as soon as you can.'

But she hadn't wanted to leave work right after the foreman called, so she stayed. Sally, her best friend and fellow employee, was leaving for a new job, a better job in another city, and Ambrosia had wanted to be there for the goodbye celebration. She had a terrific speech written up and she'd wanted to give it.

By the time she reached the hospital later that evening, it was obvious that what had happened to Tom had happened to them both.

Break time is over. Ambrosia wipes splatter marks off the mirrors in the staff washroom and thinks of Tom, stiff as a broom handle, lying on the sofa at home. Gazing into one of the mirrors she has just cleaned, she runs fingers along its bottom edge and considers her alternatives. She could move out, leave Tom to his own devices, and bear the shame of her desertion. She could travel, but choose places that are accessible so she can include Tom. She could volunteer at an animal shelter instead of getting a dog that would aggravate Tom's allergies.

Or, she thinks, with a grim little smile, maybe she'll put herself first and get herself the dog she wants anyway.

CANAL STREET CATHOUSE

The morning after the Victoria Day long weekend, Paul Dietrich hammered a *For Sale* sign into an overgrown patch of lawn in front of the Canal Street Cathouse. He had drawn the short straw by becoming the agent of record. The only saving grace was the extra two percent commission the seller had promised on top of the usual three. Paul felt it would take a miracle to sell the joint. Sandwiched between a barbershop and a boarded-up Baptist church, the shelter had been doomed since early spring. The community had failed the cats after the CEO was caught pouring donations into the local rub-and-tug massage parlour.

The shelter was like no other; the cats had the run of the place. No cages. No segregation. Just one big happy feline family.

Paul forced the key into the lock, but the door stuck firm. 'Damn it,' he said, heaving with his shoulder. 'Something for the repair list.' Paul shook his head. The first thing that hit him was the smell. While Paul was fairly certain the shelter volunteers did their best, little could mask the reek of ammonia. *Cat piss,* his father would say, *stinks to high heaven.*

The likelihood of a sale at the current asking price was next to nil.

Paul had no use for cats. Growing up on the family farm, barn cats were there to control the rodent population. His parents didn't even bother feeding them. They had dogs, of course— spoiled mutts whose raison d'être was loafing around all day on the front stoop and barking their heads off at the approach of a car—but those were pets, indulged and coddled. The cats were workers; they had to earn their own meals.

Entering the living room from the hall, all Paul could see were cats lounging on every surface. On window ledges. On sofas. On the backs of easy chairs. On the kitchen counter. On top of the stove and fridge. Fifty moist feline eyes staring at him. As Paul took it all in, it was hard to say who was more flustered, himself or the cats.

And then, when they got used to his presence, there was the noise. The incessant hissing, bawling, mewling. The constant clamour set Paul's nerves on edge. 'Shut the hell up,' he yelled at the cats. Their ears flattened, and their heads swivelled like periscopes at the sound of his voice.

Paul agreed with the commonly held belief that cats were a haughty lot. They could be such snooty little bitches, with their arched backs, their chins tilted in that ooh-la-la manner. Paul walked around the living room through the kitchen into the main floor bathroom, where many of the litter boxes stood. The cats turned toward each other as if communicating telepathically, giving him the heebie-jeebies.

A blue volunteer binder sat next to an electric can opener on the table in the kitchen. Paul knew he shouldn't snoop, but curiosity got the better of him. Inside he discovered fifty sections, one for each stray. At the top of each page was the cat's name and picture. Handy, but what a lot of work! Below that he found a full history of the cat and a list of its medical conditions and treatments. Paul wished someone with the kinds of organizational skills evident in this binder would apply at the real estate office.

Meanwhile, the cats, as cats are wont to do, figured he was about to give them food. They started roaming. He noticed one thing they all had in common: they were adept toe-walkers. He watched in awe as a cat jumped from one window ledge to another. Another cat lifted its butt toward the ceiling while its front legs extended across the kitchen counter. A third moved along the edge of a flat screen TV with the agility of a Romanian gymnast.

Paul continued to flip through the blue binder, studying the profiles for the rest of the cats. They weren't particularly young or old, although one with a grey muzzle was destined to break longevity records before long. 'That one's Dino,' Paul said to himself.

The majority of the cats looked clean and brushed. The greasy, unkempt fur of their former lives was a distant memory.

* * *

Later that week, Paul found a couple of reasons to return to the cathouse. He wished that one of those reasons was an offer to purchase, but no such luck. After Paul tweaked the hinges of the front door, he let himself in.

There'd been a complaint from one of the neighbours. The voicemail indicated that lights had flickered during the night. A dead cat, lying on the floor beside a chewed up lamp cord, told the tale. Paul poked around in the back bedrooms until he found an old empty shoebox stuffed in a closet. He brought the box back to the entry and toed the stiff corpse in before setting it and the broken lamp by the door.

He took another stroll through the shelter, his eyes keen for any other repairs that needed doing before he returned to the office. He opened the kitchen drawers. No evidence of mouse dirt. Thanks to the cats, of course.

Despite his limited feline experience, Paul thought Dino looked a little worse for wear that day. Though he didn't want to, Paul's hand found its way behind Dino's ear. The old cat's hide was rough and patchy, but Paul patted him anyway. Paul felt Dino's muscles tense beneath his fingertips before, all of a sudden, the cat began to purr. Was it just Paul's imagination or were

Dino's whiskers shorter and stubbier than he remembered? They looked as if they'd been singed by a match.

'You were a bad, bad boy, Dino. You chewed the wiring, too, didn't you?' Paul said. And then, as if Dino resented the accusation, the old cat turned his head and bit him.

Perched on an end table sat another cat the volunteers called Katrina. Her orange coat was lighter than the other tabbies at the shelter. It reminded Paul of butternut squash, and the freckles on his daughter's nose and cheeks. The notes in the volunteer binder confirmed she'd had a hard life, as evidenced by the diminished length of her tail. Paul read that she'd been found, wet and scrawny, in a gym bag next to the canal.

Katrina leapt from the table and stood by the front door, the very door Paul had repaired that morning. After pawing the front mat, she bent forward and horked up a massive hairball the colour of dead grass. 'Gross!' Paul said, flinging open every cupboard in search of paper towel and cleanser.

* * *

By mid-summer, a self-professed cat person contacted Paul about the shelter. Paul took her on a walk-through, and after her enthusiastic oohing and ahhing, the realtor predicted she might actually make an offer.

'Oh, my goodness,' the client said, 'Isn't it darling? I'll take it.'

'Great! I'll do up the paperwork this afternoon.' Paul could scarcely believe his good luck. He was finally unloading the place.

'Paperwork?'

'Or we can use my smartphone. Whatever you want.'

'Paperwork? Smartphone? For a cat?' she asked.

'Cat?'

'Yes. I'll take that one over there.' The client pointed at Isadora, whose patch of white fur formed a perfect heart around her long grey face.

By late summer, Paul had given up hope of ever dumping the shelter. Interest had definitely begun to wane. He blamed it on the holidays. People didn't want to buy when they were thinking about packing up the family for the annual camping trip or renting a cottage at the lake. That was what Paul was thinking when, out of the blue, an out-of-towner, a property developer, got in touch with him.

'The house is rumoured to be historically significant,' Paul explained. 'So you might not be able to tear the place down to put up something new.'

'I'm okay with that. I've only got a few minutes, so it'll have to be a quick run through.'

Paul had tired of going to the shelter. But there was one good thing: between his efforts and those of the remaining volunteers, the number of cats had been substantially reduced due to a surge in adoptions. Unfortunately, Paul thought, no one in their right mind would adopt Morley. Morley, such a sweet name for such a vicious looking cat. The cat resembled an evil ferret, long and lean, with gums that were almost black. The file said he had 'issues'. He couldn't resist scratching leather couches or chewing houseplants. At the end of the shelter tour, the developer stuck his hand in Morley's face.

'I wouldn't do that if I were you,' Paul said. Too late. Morley stuck his tongue out, the hooked papillae ripping into the man's skin like a rasp.

'God, I love how that feels. How much do you want for the cat?' the developer asked.

* * *

Paul's efforts to unload the cathouse were thwarted by neighbourhood brats stealing the *For Sale* sign. More times than he liked, he found the sign tossed onto the roof of the shelter. But the adoptions, at least, were continuing apace. By early fall, only two cats remained.

Simba, a black cat the size and build of a small terrier, still resided at the shelter, as did Medusa. Simba was three-legged and had white patches on his feet. Paul learned to never wear light-coloured slacks when showing the shelter, or to at least pack a lint brush in his briefcase. Man, Simba could shed. Paul figured Simba would never be adopted due to his habit of shitting on the floor next to the litter box. It never occurred to Paul—or the volunteers, for that matter—that the cause might be physical. According to the file, all efforts at behaviour modification had failed. Paul was sick and tired of picking up dried turd, the shape and texture of which was not unlike week-old Oktoberfest sausage.

Medusa had a disfigured ear. Paul had gleaned from the binder that a previous owner had tried to operate on Medusa's aural hematoma using a crochet hook. Needless to say, it didn't go well. The botched surgery had left Medusa's ear permanently bent, but despite its condition, it remained fully functional. Whenever she heard music blaring from the speakers of Paul's portable radio, Medusa jetéed around the shelter like a professionally trained dancer. In fact, she seemed to tap 'five, six, seven, eight' before skating across the linoleum.

In October, after a sudden flurry of clients had scurried through the property, Paul let himself feel hopeful he might finally hook a buyer. His hunch turned out to be right. Three potential buyers fought a vigorous bidding war. The winner demanded an end-of-October closing. As crimson leaves fluttered around him, Paul affixed a neon sticker to the sign out front. *Sold!* Finally, Paul thought. But what about Medusa and Simba?

A week before closing Paul approached the remaining volunteer about the last of the cats. She responded with a helpless shrug. 'My house is already overrun with strays. If I bring home another, my girlfriend said she'll move out.'

Paul turned the key in the lock and stood at the front door, watching Simba and Medusa groom each other. 'How sweet,' he said.

He went home, cracked open a beer, and developed a list of pros and cons. The list of pros was shorter but more compelling. It helped that Paul's wife was in full support of his idea.

It took some practice but eventually Simba's turds found their way into the litter box. Paul had cut down the height of one side and used tuna treats to reward the cat's aim. After a few sulky weeks, Medusa perked up, especially if Paul and his wife tuned the radio to the Latin music station. He suspected that what the two cats loved most about their new life was Paul's daughter. With two straps holding her upright in her electric wheelchair, she tapped her food-tray with a thumb. One by one, Medusa and Simba sprang from their perches and lined up in front of her. Leaning her head forward, Paul's daughter nuzzled each one in turn, reminding them how extraordinary they were.

THE COMPANION

It was difficult to find a euchre player to sit fourth chair at the Legion so some of the guys started seeking companions online. Glenn found one so stylish he began to dress like her—psychedelic T-shirts coupled with form-fitting jeans. Alf found himself in the companion game, too. He drove his gal all around town, the roof of his convertible folded down, his companion's hair tucked under a bright pink kerchief. Bert was amazed at how authentic the companions looked, and how they all had that new-car smell.

Bert's wife, Eunice, had made it to their forty-fifth wedding anniversary before the oncologist broke the news. After she died, Glenn and Alf offered sage advice. 'Don't make the mistake of staying alone long,' they said.

Glenn suggested Bert sell his house and move into one of those new condos by the harbour. Bert still lived in the same house where he and Eunice had raised their only child, Johanna. He wasn't interested in moving downtown. Here he had a large lot where he enjoyed pulling weeds and tending to his overgrown flower beds.

Life without Eunice soon became messy. Bert was accustomed to home-cooked meals and dessert every evening. While Johanna had assured her father she'd make sure he had enough to eat, she soon grew weary of dragging casseroles and meatloaf to her childhood home. So she left information about a service that dropped off ready-to-cook meals. All Bert would have to do would be to throw everything into a pot. He tossed the flyer out when Johanna left.

Bert usually spent his evenings in the living room, where Eunice's knitting needles and her last project still waited in the basket next to her chair. He sat there until bedtime, trying to not overthink while watching the waning sun's reflection on the hardwood floor. He'd been to the library to ask for book recommendations from the staff. There was a paperback on the table by his chair, but he found it difficult to remember the names of characters or concentrate on the plot.

One evening Bert turned on his tablet, a birthday gift from Johanna. He opened his email and hunted down the message Glenn had sent him a few weeks ago, which contained a link to the companion catalogue. It didn't take long before he stumbled upon a particularly striking specimen who went by the name Freya. He was drawn to her smile, impish yet friendly, though she had only a wisp of a mouth. She stood tall, confident, and straight. He hated when people slouched. She had broad shoulders like a swimmer. She was dressed in dark shorts and a grey tank top with broad straps and a built-in bra. There were squiggles over the fabric that reminded him of licorice nibs.

Bert couldn't stop thinking about the benefits of spending time with an aesthetically appealing robot inside of which was stored sophisticated artificial intelligence designed specially to comfort him. Something like this could be the antidote to his grief. A psychological salve without the negatives that come with finding someone to spend time with and developing a relationship with that person.

Bert held the tablet up to his face and examined Freya more intently. He admired the barrette holding the pile of auburn hair on top of her head. It was impossible to tell from the picture what her manners were like or what her voice sounded like. He loved to talk but knew it was best to allow other people to have a turn to speak especially at the start of things. He hoped Freya was a good conversationalist. He wondered if she had ever worked as a model or an actor.

Why weren't there buttons to click for more information? He had a notion to contact the manufacturer and suggest that to them. But he had already decided; nothing could stop him now. He turned on the light and opened the drawer where he kept his wallet. He scrolled down until he found the product number that corresponded with his choice of companion. There were options to specify hair colour, size, and complexion. His fingertip hovered over the price—$6,500 plus taxes and shipping. Mighty steep, so he selected the lease-to-own option. Before he had a change of heart, he entered his credit card information and clicked submit.

On Friday morning a large cardboard box appeared on his front porch. The courier asked Bert to sign the electronic receipt. 'Third one of these I've delivered this month,' he said, winking.

Bert dragged the box over the hardwood into the breakfast nook and left it there. He suddenly wondered whether the companion might be a disservice to Eunice's memory. Every evening, instead of watching the sun reflect off the hardwood, he sat in the living room where he had a perfect view of the box. He studied the cardboard, wondering if he should take advantage of the return window and send the thing back. Only the friends whose wives had died understood, really grasped, the loneliness he was experiencing. Everyone else just went on with their lives. It wasn't as if Bert could or wanted to replace Eunice. It wasn't that. He just wanted someone around he could do things with, to take on walks or to a performance at the Roxy.

After a week, he found the courage to tear open a corner of the box, squeeze his hand in, and tug the reluctant owner's manual from a plastic sleeve. He read the manual front to back to review the best way to maintain the battery-operated device— avoid immersing companion in water, replace batteries semiannually, wipe exterior with a damp cloth, and keep product away from too much sunlight.

A few more days passed before the push to open the box overwhelmed him. Using an X-Acto knife, he sliced through the packing tape and released Freya into his life. He could have sworn he heard her say *What took you so long? You ordered me so here I am,* but that was impossible. He hadn't yet activated the ON switch at the back of her neck.

Bert poured over the owner's manual again, in case he'd missed anything during his first read-through. It took less than an hour for Freya's built-in computer to configure itself. She slipped from the confines of the box all on her own and immediately got to work. She found the kitchen, fixed him a snack, and brewed some coffee.

After some initial awkwardness, he found he liked having a companion. It was so convenient, and he believed Freya was just the thing to bring him out of his grief. The companion made her way around with the confidence of someone who'd spent years in his kitchen. No worming through the drawers in search of a spatula or can opener—she instantly committed the contents of the cupboards and pantry to memory. After his snack, Bert set his fork and knife next to his plate. Without Bert needing to ask, Freya whisked everything away before drawing him a bath. How did she know he loved a long soak in the afternoon?

Later, Bert told Freya he felt like taking a nap. When pressed, she admitted she was exhausted from travelling from the distribution centre in Sacramento to his house. Bert showed her to the guest room before heading off to his room.

Soon Bert and Freya settled into a routine. Meals, light conversation, and quiet times, during which he managed to rekindle his interest in reading. She liked needlepoint or completing the crossword on the back pages of the newspaper. One evening, after a meal of prime rib, roast potatoes, and shredded broccoli salad, they strolled to the harbour and back. Anyone running into them would presume they were a nice couple in the throes of a loving relationship.

Bert took care to not walk too far ahead like he so often did with his wife—and for which Eunice often chastised him. Freya, with her lean legs and long stride, was able to keep up no problem. Bert was shocked they hadn't managed to run into anyone he knew. It was too soon to introduce her to his circle of friends and former colleagues. Alf and Glenn had both waited before springing their companions on the gang at the Legion. They had explained that taking time to bond with their companions had been time well spent.

Bert, who loved a good tale, liked learning about Freya. How she liked to read real-life stories, not made-up ones. That she'd acquired her love of needlepoint from her grandmother on her father's side. How she wished she could keep a tune.

After their walk, they shared raspberry scones and chai tea, a drink she'd brought into his life. The moment seemed right for Bert to say, 'You make me happy.'

'I'm getting accustomed to being here, too,' Freya said, her eyes wide and wet.

He wondered at how quickly his feelings for Freya had developed. It seemed she'd barely arrived in his life and she was already growing on him. He liked how she'd helped revive his zest and enthusiasm for life.

'Where would you be if you weren't here?' Bert asked.

'I'm not sure I understand,' said Freya. 'There is only here.'

'Never mind. Just know that I'm happy now, happier than I have a right to be, happier than perhaps I've ever been.' He wasn't sure why he added the last part. It seemed a slight against his dead wife. Even prior to becoming ill, Eunice had started to become matronly. It was sad. She'd tired of doing her hair or brushing her cheeks with a bit of blush. And she'd started to complain about the normal aches and pains that came with aging. He had loved her anyway, but his happiness had felt dulled by her neglect.

'It's good that you are becoming accustomed to me.'

'And you don't mind being stuck here with an old man like me?'

'Why would I mind? This is my place in life.'

Days went by. Weeks. Months. Christmas was fast approaching. While Freya shopped for the required seasonal items to complete their celebration, Bert called up his friends. First Glenn, then Alf. With Freya in his life, Bert rarely made time to stop by the Legion. The guys were desperate to know when Bert might bring Freya around so they could meet her. 'Not yet,' Bert said, stalling. 'She's kind of shy. You two making a fuss over her might be too much.'

Bert's ears filled with their questions. What was she like? Did she have a favourite colour? What did she like to cook? Did she have any hobbies? Had they done it yet? It hadn't occurred to Bert that they might *do it*. He wanted a companion, not a sexual partner. Although he wasn't averse to the idea of becoming intimate with Freya, it had to be a mutual decision, a determination that they arrived at together.

Johanna arrived mid-morning on Christmas Day. She was wearing Eunice's green leather jacket, her pale, freckled face a shocking contrast to the dark fur collar. Bert remembered the day that Johanna had asked if she could have the jacket. He hadn't, at the time, known how he felt about it, but now he was happy Johanna took pleasure in keeping a part of Eunice close to her.

Her childhood home smelled of turkey, sage, and squash, all the fixings. 'I didn't know you could cook like this, Dad,' Johanna said. 'You always said the prep was too messy, but it was fine if Mom did it.'

Rather than get into it with her, he stood and turned toward his bedroom.

'Dad! Don't ignore me.'

He really didn't want to have this conversation with Johanna, so he retrieved her gift, something Freya had picked up at the mall. It was a diamond and gold bangle bracelet with Johanna's name engraved inside. Johanna pointed out that the engraver had omitted the 'h' in her name.

'Damn. I wished I'd checked that. I'm sorry, honey.'

Johanna waved it off, saying people misspelled it all the time. She gave Bert an old-fashioned sled and a wreath of pine boughs, something to brighten the space by the front door.

Bert drew in a deep breath before patting the space beside him on the couch. 'Sit next to me, Johanna. I have something to tell you.' He reached for her hand. 'There's someone new in my life. A companion.'

Johanna fell back as if she'd been struck. 'So soon? Mom hasn't even been gone a year.'

Bert's hands folded around each other, seeking strength. 'Part of me died when your mother passed. I cried every day that first month after we buried her. It broke me, her empty pillow next to mine.

'Dad, I'm so sorry. I wish she were here, too, more than you could know. But I'm glad to hear that you've started dating.'

'Actually, I'm not dating. She's here. Let me go get her.' Bert stepped into the kitchen and dragged Freya out. It seemed she had a shy side after all.

'What the hell! A plastic sex doll?' Johanna's voice shook with disbelief.

'The proper term is full-service companion,' he said.

'Dad, she's a robot, a plastic toy, nothing more than an overpriced mannequin,' she said, shaking her head in disgust.

'Since you want to get all technical, you should know that Freya isn't plastic. She's constructed with a polyvinyl chloride skeleton and has articulated steel—'

'Mom must be rolling over in her grave.'

Bert didn't know what to say.

'Is her hair real? Like from a donor?' Johanna's eyebrows lifted in horror.

'Of course it's real. It's organically grown,' he said, letting out an audible sigh. 'Why in the world would you wonder such a thing? What does it matter?' Freya's hair reminded him of Eunice's before hers fell out.

'Dad, I gave you the tablet, so you could connect with people online, but I was thinking of real life human beings. Not ... this.' Johanna waved a disapproving hand in Freya's direction.

Freya said, 'Perhaps I should leave—'

'You stay right there, Freya! Johanna and I, we're done here.' Bert retrieved Johanna's jacket and hat from the tree stand and held them out.

'But, Dad, we haven't even eaten.'

Bert opened the door.

'You're choosing a doll over me, your own flesh and blood?' Johanna asked, pulling on the jacket.

'I suppose you're right.'

Icy rain streamed down for the remainder of the afternoon. The bitter dampness seeped through the walls and into Bert's bones, leaving him achy, miserable, and filled with regret. What had he done? Perhaps he shouldn't have been so short with Johanna, but she'd been the one to make a mockery of him.

His irritation leached into January, his mood grey as the mounds of dirty snow along the driveway and street. Freya was always there with a smile on her face. Her deportment and manner were pleasant enough, but Bert detected a difference in her attitude. Her smile seemed too broad, her deportment and manner *too* pleasant.

As he drilled down and observed her closely throughout their morning routine, he found what he'd suspected all along. She did not express interest or excitement, but nor did she complain. She continued to cook his meals, clean up after them, converse with him, but he no longer felt the thrill of her company, the happiness he had felt only months ago. He'd always suspected it would happen: Freya had grown bored of him.

Bert hated to admit it, but he'd been suffering from ennui as well. This wasn't something he could bring up with Alf or Glenn, who were both still crazy about their chosen companions. Perhaps it was the model he'd selected. If only he'd taken more care when initially deciding. His rush to replace Eunice had caused him to select blindly. Freya was a dud, a lemon from which he could no longer make lemonade.

He wished Freya were more of a conversationalist, but how deeply could they go when she never read a newspaper or listened to the radio. She was unable to offer an opinion on a paint colour for the living room, let alone politics or culture. He thought that her agreeableness and familiarity were what he'd wanted but he'd been wrong. Her answers were robotic in tone and content. It had taken him so long to notice.

He'd offered to pay for lessons—scrapbooking, voice lessons, glass blowing, whatever she wanted—but she couldn't be bothered. She never argued when he selected a TV program for them to watch, nor did she care about the music he chose from his extensive CD collection. She'd taken to disappearing to her bedroom after breakfast and not coming out until she had to make the next meal.

Ever since their fight at Christmas, Johanna had stayed away, too. Oh, how Bert pined for her company. She was polite enough to answer his text messages, but only if he texted first or asked a question. She never made the first move. Something was wrong. His hopes that Freya would extinguish his loneliness had only caused deeper heartache.

'I've disappointed you,' Freya said one night after a meal of pork tenderloin, pickled beets, garlic mashed potatoes, and crème brûlée. 'Perhaps the food is lacking?'

'Oh, gosh no. No, it's not that. If I'm candid, I have felt disappointment, but not with you. This arrangement between us simply isn't working. You'll have to go, find somewhere new.'

'The lease agreement runs out on the third of next month,' Freya said, peering at the readout on the inside of her wrist. 'At that time if you want I'll simply vanish from your life.'

By the first of March, balmier weather had blown in, a break from the mind-numbing chill of deep winter. Bert and Freya strolled along the harbour arm-in-arm, tossing crusts to the ducks paddling in the murky water below. With only a couple of days before her planned departure, Bert found he'd begun to enjoy being with Freya again, to appreciate her light company, easy ways, and thin conversation. Perhaps their little arrangement might work out after all.

On their last night together, Bert cooked. He prepared freshwater fish, coleslaw with balsamic vinaigrette, and home fries, simple recipes he'd learned watching a cooking show. They both ate with hearty enthusiasm and consumed far too much wine. Before Bert knew it, his head thumped to the table, where he slept away the night.

He awoke to a cleared table and early morning sunshine streaming in from an east-facing window. He called out but received no response. He found the guest room tidy, the bed made, the closet cleaned out, Freya's boots and coat gone. He listened for footsteps but there were none. No sign of life. She hadn't even left a note. It was really over. Bert sat alone, no breakfast on a plate in front of him, no smell of bacon in the air. The house felt empty. He wanted to call Johanna. It was high time he asked her to come over. On the other hand, perhaps all he needed was a companion upgrade—one that could at least carry a tune. He leaned forward and reached for his tablet.

THE COLLECTORS

So far I'd failed to dig up anything significant about the mysterious disappearance of the woman who lived across the street from where I now stood. I plodded through the snow toward the small house in front of me. Unless this next interview went better than the rest there'd be no story, and without a story my editor would hand me my ass on a porcelain platter. After a final flicker of hesitation, I pressed the doorbell. Behind textured glass, a large, blurry figure fumbled with the lock and cracked open the door.

'I called earlier.' I dangled my *Herald-Times* ID in front of the woman's closely spaced blue eyes.

'I'm Miss Gold. You want my grandmother. She just stepped out.' As Miss Gold spoke, there were long pauses between her words as she struggled to catch her breath.

'Actually, would you mind if I started with you?'

Miss Gold wore oversized blue scrubs and gave off a peppery smell. Two half-moon armpit stains discoloured her shirt. I assumed she'd been using the stationary bike I spied at the end of the hall.

'Mind if I come in?' I gestured at the snow spinning with the fury of a piñata spitting candy.

Miss Gold's eyes fluttered briefly before she fully opened the door. She insisted I leave my boots on. I shadowed her into a dim, overheated sitting area. She turned on a lamp. I shrugged off my coat but left on my toque to hide my hat hair.

'It's my understanding that 425 Veronica Street has stood

empty for a while.' As I pulled my notebook from my satchel, the interstate thrummed with midafternoon traffic.

Miss Gold tugged at her shirt collar before clicking her neck left and right. 'Then you know as much as anyone else does about that cursed place.'

She folded and refolded a crumpled tissue she'd mined from somewhere. I glanced at my notebook hoping I might get her to expand upon the only juicy tidbit of information I had.

'I understand the previous owner, Mrs Layton, had a—'

'Yes, a lover. A woman, in fact,' Miss Gold said.

'They say the place is—'

'Haunted? Honestly, wait and ask Bubbe. I don't know anything about it.'

I glanced out the window. Third day in a row of grisly January weather. I couldn't wait to book a vacation—for anywhere but here. But first I had to find a story. I needed a different approach.

'Could I bother you for a cup of coffee? It's freezing outside.'

I trailed Miss Gold down the hallway to the kitchen and tapped the bike. 'I should start a fitness program.'

'Oh, I don't ride. We're storing it.'

She gestured for me to sit on a chair next to the sliding door that overlooked the porch.

'Shoot,' she said into the open cupboard. 'We're out of instant. Tea okay?'

'Whatever you're having.'

While the kettle boiled, she pushed aside an empty soup can and a couple of prescription bottles to reach a turquoise teapot. She plucked two teabags out of a ceramic canister and dropped them in the pot, pouring in the hot water and letting it steep for a moment. I looked out the sliding door and watched as birds fluttered around a near-empty feeder.

When Miss Gold poured, a pungent pong rose from my cup.

I blew across the steamy liquid. Despite the strong odour, the concoction offered a spicy yet soothing flavour. 'What did you say the tea is called?'

'I didn't. It's a family secret.' Laughter bubbled up and out of her as if from a youngster with slander to spread about the popular kid in class.

'Join me?' I asked.

'Perhaps later.' We were interrupted by the sound of the garage door rasping along its track. Miss Gold turned in the direction of the noise. 'She's home.'

Miss Gold's grandmother, a short woman with a chunky build, appeared. Her yellow down-filled jacket and fuchsia pants were as bright as candy floss.

'Who's walking with wet boots? You think I have all day to clean?' She swivelled her gaze toward me. 'They call me Bubbe.'

'This is the reporter you were expecting,' said Miss Gold pointing an accusing hand at me. When she bent to lift the groceries, sweat oiled her face. I considered lending a hand but how had she helped me? Instead I asked to use the bathroom.

When I returned, Bubbe pointed at the pill bottles on the counter. 'She lazy. Ever since she must take those.'

Someone had left the doors to the floor-to-ceiling pantry ajar. Instead of food, every conceivable kind of footwear filled the shelves. Timberland boots. T-strap sandals. Oxfords. Sneakers. Heels back, toes out. Pumps. Work boots. Wedge heels. Docksides. Different sizes, all arranged with care. Jelly shoes. Mary Janes. Crocs. Moccasins. Rubber boots. Not your typical storage space for shoes and boots.

'You have boarders?' I asked, pointing at the pantry.

'Oh, no. I'm a collector.' Miss Gold shut the doors.

Compared to the cold outside, the house was unbearably hot and stuffy. My body felt weak and limp, like a soggy sandwich. I hoped I wasn't coming down with that bug that was going around. I collapsed into my chair.

'Hats off!' Bubbe tore my toque from my head.

'Ouch!' I rubbed my scalp.

'Not good to wear in house,' Bubbe said. 'You here about warm sisters?'

'Warm sisters?' I scribbled the expression into my notebook.

Metal clanged against a flagpole as Miss Gold stooped to top up my cup. 'You know, kissy-faces.'

Miss Gold pulled at her shirt. 'Bubbe, watch out or she'll write that you called Mrs Layton silly names.'

'She talk yet, about them?' Bubbe nodded at her granddaughter.

'Not really. I'd hoped—' My tongue wilted against my bottom teeth.

Bubbe's brow furrowed before she cocked an eyebrow in the direction of Miss Gold. 'Soft in head since breakup with crazy boyfriend, do nothing all day.'

Miss Gold said, 'My boyfriend isn't crazy.'

I shook my head. The heat in the room was making me drowsy, and I could barely keep my eyes open.

'The neighbours?' I asked. 'You mean Mrs Layton and—'

Bubbe studied the floor for answers. 'Mrs Layton everyday outside, clean, polish, rake leaf. All the time shovel, even in snowstorm.' She twirled a finger at her temple.

'Everyone shovels,' Miss Gold said.

'TV says blizzard coming, Mrs Layton push shovel. Girlfriend at window like a ghost. Every time look, do nothing.'

'Ghost?' I said.

'Bubbe, I must have told you a million times, 425 Veronica isn't haunted.'

'She no wear boots.'

'What?' I asked.

'No boots.' Outside, the bird feeder spun like a wind sock.

Miss Gold said, 'You shouldn't speak ill of—'

'What? It's not hush-hush. Everyone know,' Bubbe said, rubbing her hands in front of her.

'Knows what?' I asked.

Miss Gold sighed. 'Mrs Layton wore Crocs.'

'In the winter?' I looked at the handmade mukluks I'd bought on a trip to the Arctic. They'd cost me an entire week's pay.

'Girlfriend,' Bubbe said. 'She no care. She inside, other works like slave.'

'Mrs Layton wasn't a slave.'

'What else?'

I became aware of a maddening buzz in my ears.

This wasn't much of a story. If only I could pay attention long enough to wrap up the interview and crawl home to bed.

Bubbe's lips formed a line of concern. 'She *nafka*, no?'

Miss Gold poured more tea. 'A whore? Bubbe, be nice.'

The words in my notebook jiggled there, unrecognizable gibberish. My brain was sponge toffee.

'She was in nightshirt,' Bubbe said, her exhales strident and deliberate. 'No coat. Hat off. No mittens.'

'You mean the one in the window?'

'No! Mrs Layton,' Bubbe and Miss Gold said at once.

Here we were at the kitchen table, a trio of gossips wasting an afternoon together, only nothing made sense. Who would venture into sub-zero temperatures scantily clad to please their partner, male or female? One good thing: the special tea had grown on me. I'd have to ask if I could buy some. But what I truly wanted was to sandwich myself between my mattress and duvet and sleep for a year.

And then it hit me—the footwear in the pantry. Miss Gold had identified herself as a collector. It reminded me of that movie about the creepy guy who collected butterflies and little girls. Didn't people with shoe fetishes want to wear what they hoarded? Then why the different sizes? There were even baby shoes.

Things weren't adding up. Filled with the urge to leave once and for all, I pushed myself to a wobbly upright position.

'She didn't tell?' Bubbe's words sliced the air as she pointed a gnarly knuckle at her granddaughter. 'She do, what is it?' She creased a hand over the other and pumped the air.

Miss Gold made a harrumph sound while her neck lengthened with self-importance. 'I performed CPR.'

Bubbe's fingers drummed the table. 'Put that in story.'

'*You* saved Mrs Layton?' Miss Gold had certainly undersold herself earlier. I had difficulty picturing her with the wherewithal to revive anyone.

'I shouldn't have bothered.' Her words echoed strangely in the space between us. 'All my efforts wasted. She died right there on the sidewalk.'

I promised to check again for a police report. Something wasn't jiving. If Miss Gold was the last one to see Mrs Layton alive, why was this the first time I'd heard of it? I'd interviewed everyone on the block and no one had mentioned a thing about Mrs Layton receiving CPR. No one had even seen a dead body. With my elbows on the table, I folded my fingers into a tent and perched my chin there.

'Good thing we were home, her, me.' A smirk creased Bubbe's otherwise stern face. 'You put our names in paper?'

'I'll ask my—' My voice was barely a whisper, a searing pain sprouting behind my eyes.

'Me, you, her, we're not same.'

'You're right.' Miss Gold's eyes flashed. 'We're not tattletales.'

The words didn't even register. Did Mrs Layton's girlfriend by the window even exist? Was Mrs Layton actually dead? I didn't have much, but maybe I had enough to convince my editor something was up. The collector angle was an added bonus. Could be the makings of a human-interest feature. I'd have to return and take some photos.

Miss Gold made a game of opening and closing the faucet. 'If only I'd gotten Mrs Layton to drink the tea straight up.'

Then it hit me. Mrs Layton had been wearing Crocs. I had seen a pink pair front and centre in the pantry. What if they were hers? I was overcome by a feeling of being trapped. Suddenly it seemed I'd walked into something sinister. I felt like an imposter, completely out of my league, trying to unearth a story from two unreliable witnesses. If only I could scrub the brain fog that had taken over my mind. Did I ever need a holiday.

I began to cry, but someone yelled for me to stop. I cowered at the sight of a fist, ready to smack me. Heads belonging to Miss Gold and Bubbe became as big as gigantic balloons. The women floated around me on invisible trays. They were smiling, their teeth serrated blades. Miss Gold bent over me and stuffed a sock into my mouth. I gagged and then couldn't breathe. I grabbed at pasty-white maggots, their jaws digging into my face, but my fingers came away empty. As I slid to the floor, Miss Gold and Bubbe shrieked with delight as they ripped the mukluks clean off my feet.

IN HONOUR OF MIRIAM

The stink of rotten meat hits Walt as he steps from his Jeep into the two-car garage. Miriam's goddamned fly traps. She blames Walt for the flies, saying that's what he gets for leaving the garage door open. The type of trap Miriam sets is rudimentary in design, and flawlessly effective. Chicken gizzards fill the base of a Mason jar. Flies plunge headfirst through tiny slits in the lid. In the course of a week, a single female deposits 600 eggs, leaving maggots to seethe on the decomposing flesh. Mature flies then fritter away their lives endlessly banging their heads against the lid.

When he enters the kitchen, Walt calls out Miriam's name like he always does, his flinty voice echoing off the cathedral ceiling. And, like he does after every trip into town, he climbs the stairs and stands in the doorway of her studio. He loves to watch her work. Only Miriam isn't there.

If she were, she would be smearing adhesive onto a life-size clay sculpture. She'd be attaching found objects such as hieroglyphics, musical score, and postage stamps to form a story about the woman who had commissioned the work. Always the upper body: chest, breasts, abdomen. Yet each sculpture made unique by the woman's individual body type, breast shape and size, and selected adornments. The pungent odour of glue and paint rides the studio air despite Miriam's absence.

With his big toe, Walt nudges the stool where she used to sit, remembering how he would stand behind her and lift a tangle of hair from her shoulders as she manipulated clay. How, when he stooped to plant a kiss, a hint of vanilla-scented body spray would mix with her natural musty smell. A scent that caused him to sigh with regret.

Walt has been to the doctor twice since Miriam's funeral. The complaint is an old one: that he can't sleep. The doctor cautioned Walt to ease off caffeine and avoid exercising at night. She said, 'You need to get on with your life. There's such a thing as grieving too long.'

'You make it sound easy.' Walt's trembling hands did a worry dance in front of his chest.

'Did I mention this already? No more naps. That's the worst thing you can do. I'll start you on a light sleeping medication to help you over the hump.' She scribbled something illegible on a prescription pad.

Walt keeps some things from the doctor. That he hears Miriam's voice. That he sees her standing on the concession road when he goes to fetch the mail. Walt worries that if he mentions any of this, the doctor will diagnose him with something worse than grief.

Yet, even with the support of sleeping medication, instead of feeling well rested, Walt feels groggy with the memory of nightmares that drag on into the next day. For the first time in his life, he dreads the night and going to bed. Cut flowers, now discoloured in their glass vases, line the dresser where he and Miriam kept their intimates. (Her word, not his.) He doesn't have the strength to toss the flowers out, nor can he face the stack of sympathy cards on the windowsill.

All those people at the funeral home, the line snaking through the foyer, past the video loop of Miriam's life. All those people, hugging him, patting him on the shoulder, their faces making it clear they can't believe Miriam is gone. So sudden. So unexpected. So blah, blah, blah. All that sympathy, yet not one person has rushed to his side. Not a single one.

He hammers wool blankets over the bedroom windows to keep out the blazing sun. He thinks about Miriam every second of the day. He has recently taken to wearing her pyjamas, the ones with the dolphins that she sewed herself. Despite them being baggier than what he'd normally wear, he pulls the drawstring tight until they fit. When he wears them, he can feel her skin next to his.

He worries about his breathing, how it has changed. There was a time when Walt had been able to run. Nothing as ambitious as a marathon, but he had been known to undertake a strenuous jog to town and back. Now all he can do is pant. His breathing, especially on the inhale, is frayed, like a chest cold without the cough. His arms feel heavy, too, like he has been stacking cords of firewood for hours on end. He's in such a weakened state that he can barely lift Miriam's journals.

Strange. After all these years that he was unaware of her writing habit.

There are four books in total. He piles them on her desk and studies a sketch of the sculpture she last worked on. She had been helping another cancer patient preserve what had been. A survivor of a double mastectomy. One day the woman had two beautiful breasts; the next, only scar tissue and emptiness.

* * *

The night before the accident, Miriam and Walt had bickered. Nothing serious. A recurring theme, actually. He'd been at the pool where he volunteered with the Special Olympics. His team consisted of two visually impaired swimmers, one a ten-year-old boy and the other a teenage girl.

'You're late. Third time this week,' Miriam said as soon as he stepped into the studio.

He checked the time on the clock. Shortly past ten. Not this again. The silent treatment. Walt despised fighting. It wasn't like

Miriam wasn't justified—admittedly, in the early years of their marriage, Walt had made his share of passes at anything with a bit of a wiggle.

'We went for ice cream.'

Walt's eyes collided with Miriam's for a moment. Hers were dark and distant, like buttons on an old coat. 'How is your little blind girlfriend?'

'Miriam, you can't be serious!'

'You spend more time with her than me.' Her hands fussed with a rag, folding and refolding. 'You probably like the idea of that sightless girl touching you down there.'

'Don't be ridiculous!'

He shuddered. She was right. There were times Walt had felt himself stiffen as he watched the girl towel herself off. And he'd felt himself react again as he watched her tongue probe her ice cream cone.

'And don't forget the boy,' he said. 'I took them both to Dairy Queen.'

'That's what you always say.' She turned away.

Walt began to reach out a hand in a gesture of good faith, but thought better of it. When she got stuck, there was no reasoning her out of it. She circled around him and hurled expletives until her voice turned hoarse. No amount of 'yeah, buts' would convince her that there was nothing between him and the swimmer. It was strange. Miriam hadn't even met the girl with eye sockets that resembled withered petunias.

Miriam and Walt went their separate ways that night, he to their bedroom and she to her studio where she kept a cot. Walt was confident Miriam would come around. She usually did.

Only this time was different.

When he awoke the next morning, Miriam was gone, en route to her mother's. Then, a few hours later, a police cruiser pushed up the laneway. The officer said a dump truck missed a bend in the road and plowed right into her. He assured Walt that Miriam hadn't felt a thing.

* * *

One month after the funeral, Walt's neighbour, Chantal, presses his doorbell.

'I thought you'd never answer,' she said, leaning against the porch railing. 'I need your wood splitter. For the summer solstice party.' Chantal steps forward and hands a handmade poster to Walt. Near the top of the paper is a crayon sketch of a large yellow sun. It looked like the kind of drawing a little kid would do.

Walt feels like crying. There's no reason in particular. Because Chantal is there and Miriam is not. Because the doorbell rang and Miriam wasn't home to answer it. Because he hates that Miriam will never again make tiramisu. Because his wife is dead, and no one but Walt seems to notice or care.

Walt doesn't care much for Chantal. Her over-the-top enthusiasm, her spiky hair, her nose and ears with more piercings than he could count, and that wiry hair on her legs, more like whiskers than something that should grow on a woman. He looks at her face, her plump pomegranate lips and says, 'This isn't a good time.'

Chantal reaches out and takes hold of his arm, likely as a gesture of kindness. But he finds her grip bossy, the weight of it too much. Without thinking, he gives her a shove, enough to cause her to lose her footing on the porch.

'What the fuck, Walt! We're only trying to help.'

Walt wants Chantal to leave. He wants to go back inside and sit quietly with his wife's journals. He feels himself shifting, like he's standing on ball bearings. 'Take the splitter and go,' he manages to say. He closes the door, letting the solstice party invitation drift away.

Upstairs in Miriam's studio, Walt opens another journal. Its cover is beige with streaks of orange and turquoise. The swirls of colour remind him of the inside of a marble. Most of the pages are empty except for a word or phrase. On some she has drawn stick figures with a Sharpie. Pictures of goats, horses, and other farm animals. An angel. The blade of a garden tool. He doesn't pretend to understand.

Near the back of the book the pages feel sticky. The drawings are tube-like, purplish in hue, veined. One looks like a penis or perhaps a snake. He wonders if he ever really knew Miriam.

During one of Walt's recent visits to the medical clinic, his doctor shared that in cases of intense melancholy, it's best to establish a semblance of routine. Like Miriam who according to the dates running along the top of the journal pages had been regularly recording in journals for years yet never thought to mention it. He wonders if there are more hidden away somewhere in the house, in the attic, or at the back of her studio closet. If there are other things he doesn't know about her. If she touched herself while drawing the penis-like shapes, such strange, dirty little pictures if you asked him. He doesn't know how he couldn't have known everything about his wife after all their years together.

* * *

The weekend of the solstice party arrives. Verdant leaves flutter on the trees dotting Walt's property. A tractor trailer carrying Porta Potties zips past on the concession road, loose gravel clinking against the undercarriage. On the kitchen radio, an announcer natters on about the weather, a weekend blessed with an idyllic forecast. 'This weekend, solstice enthusiasts will assemble along the highest ridges, drums jammed between their knees, to welcome the longest day of the year. Come on out and celebrate. By the way, for the linguists out there, the word "drum" is Irish for "ridge".' Walt flicks off the radio.

Miriam hated large social events, but if she were here, she'd be telling Walt they had to make an appearance. She'd insist that's what good neighbours do.

Walt has no intention of being a good neighbour. He's in no mood for a party. Besides, it would be presumptuous of him to think the notice Chantal left was an invitation. That she expected or wanted him to show his face. It doesn't escape him that Miriam would have formulated any excuse to snoop.

In years gone by, as a younger married couple, he and Miriam would try to stay up as long as possible on the longest day of the year. They would sit around a campfire. She'd imbibe on a couple of glasses of hard apple cider, him on beer. They shared a ritual at this high point of the year, something she'd come up with, to honestly share what the past six months had meant to them. If their winter dreams had been fulfilled. What had grown that it needed harvesting. It was all very airy-fairy and kind of silly but for a few years, it brought them closer together and a modicum of pleasure. A connection. But, like so many other things in long-term relationships, this ritual faded away over time and was replaced with apathy and boredom.

Before the first tent has been erected, the faint sound of drums filters through the air. Despite his intention to forget the solstice party, Walt feels an urge to train his eyes on the ridge where the gathering is set to take place. He heads off in search of a ladder. Field glasses dangle from his neck as he leans his extension ladder against the eaves. He climbs up and trains the binoculars on the hill, a thumb toggling the focus.

'Holy cow!'

Hundreds of oil barrels speckle the hill. Mobs of people surround the barrels, clutching wooden mallets and banging on them with wild, joyful abandon. As day turns to night, the clamour of the drums grows louder and louder, leaving Walt shaking with irritation. Suddenly, a crash like kibbles pattering against a steel bowl sets his teeth on edge. A mosquito probes his back, in a spot he can't reach. Across the way, beams of light slice the dark as mothers, clutching the hands of their youngsters, line up for the Porta Potties. When the drumming can't get any louder, it's replaced by a shrill hum.

There's no escaping the stench of kerosene riding the smoke. If Miriam were standing beside him, she'd be whispering, *What if cinders escape and ignite the woodlot? You'd better stay up and watch,* she'd insist.

But Walt is not afraid. He climbs down from his perch, heads inside, and swallows a couple of sleeping pills.

After he wriggles into Miriam's pyjamas, he curls atop the mattress. He wraps his pillow around his head to muffle the racket and coaxes his tongue to sit freely in his mouth. He breathes the way the doctor taught him. One breath in. Hold. Exhale. Relax.

* * *

The next morning his armpits smell sour and his joints are stiff, but there's no sleeping pill hangover. Outside the window, a storm is brewing. Only it's not thunder he hears; it's that idiotic drumming again.

'Jesus Murphy, shut the hell up!'

He has a quick breakfast before climbing onto his riding mower, an attempt to drown out the drums. After mowing the grass around the house, he guides the machine along the patch of grass that grows next to the concession road.

A twinkle from the ditch catches his eye. A six-pack of Stella, a decent foreign beer. He smiles, the first time in weeks. He feels alive, like the grief that has gripped him might actually fade one day. He feels he hasn't had a turn in his luck in so long.

Down the road Walt spots a man leaning against a fence post. He's wrinkly with grey whiskers and a ponytail and a face riddled with pockmarks. Walt hops off the lawnmower and walks towards him. Even from a distance, he can see that the man's eyes are the same colour as Miriam's, but bloodshot. A bongo drum rests in the grass on the ground next to the man's leg.

'Help you?' Walt says.

'Nope.'

'This is private property, you know.'

'Oh, sorry, man.' He makes no effort to move but gestures toward the ridge. 'I'm too old for this.'

'Me, too,' Walt says, considering the joint the man holds out to him. In return, Walt removes a bottle of Stella from the mower. 'Something you left behind?'

* * *

After Walt finishes the lawn, he heads for the kitchen. He slaps together a peanut butter sandwich before taking the stairs two at a time up to Miriam's studio. He opens another of her journals, its pages thick and rigid against his fingers. There are postcards glued here and there along with folded newspaper clippings with local police reports and obituaries of people he had no idea she knew. One obituary had a star next to it: Frank Hoy.

This name he does know. Her high school sweetheart, until Walt swayed her to date him.

Why had she kept it from him, the fact that she still thought about Frank? Walt wouldn't have cared. That thing with Frank was so long ago.

From the ridge, the mob releases a coyote shriek.

He grips the journals in his hands, two in each. When he'd stumbled upon them only a few days before, they'd felt heavy, but now they're metaphorically lighter. He's grateful he found them. He won't, can't, go back to the past. That was a maze without an out. He puts the journals back down.

He feels a further rush of energy. He wants to do something, leave a mark, but how? What? He rummages through a drawer of paints, selects a few tubes, holds them in his hands, studies them.

He squirts dollops of colour on the smooth surface of the otherwise grey clay form—Miriam's last, unfinished sculpture. He spreads the paint with his fingers, mimics what he'd seen Miriam do a million times, smearing pigment and creating texture. His arms feel loose and free as he adds anchors, waves, and seagulls to build a narrative. When he squints, he detects flecks and symbols Miriam had left on the clay. Dashes, a series of indecipherable letters and numbers, and question marks. A part of her remains in this work.

Scalloped clouds scud past the open studio window, streaking the walls with shadows of the coming storm. But Walt doesn't care; he has finished his wife's final work by making his own marks. Building toward a crescendo, the drumming stops at the precise moment Bert applies his final brushstroke. The work of art is pleasing relief from the ache of his grief.

The stink of kerosene fills his nostrils. Using an elbow, he slams the window closed.

In the kitchen he pops open a Stella before heading for the porch. The crowd on the ridge has thinned out, their ear-splitting impact on the weekend a mere memory.

He slips the joint from his pocket and holds it in front of him. If Miriam were here, she'd say *hurry up and share it with me.*

He moistens the rolling paper with his tongue and flicks the wheel on his lighter. He inhales deeply in honour of Miriam.

THREADBARE SMILE

Robert would deny until the day he died that the long drive from the old-age home to the hunting camp combined with his lung cancer had left him in a weakened state. While rain pimpled the windshield, he pressed his back against the passenger seat of his son's pickup and tucked his arthritic hands under his thighs. A few minutes later, Brady pulled into an overgrown laneway and set the parking brake. He walked around the front of the truck, then opened the passenger door. When he held a hand out to his father, Robert pushed it away.

'Don't baby me. I can damn well get out on my own.'

'Mind your step,' Brady said, ignoring his father.

Robert pointed at the corroded running board. 'You ought to get that replaced sometime. A man could fall and break his—'

'I know, Pop. That's why I'm trying to help you out.'

Brady wished, not for the first time, that he could speak his mind to his father. Perhaps then he would have been able to tell Robert how much he hated the idea of this hunting trip and the solitude it imposed on the two of them. How much he wanted to avoid Robert's growling and snapping, even though this could be the last time they were able to make the trip together. But as long as Brady could remember, he'd been unable to stand up to his father's commanding presence.

If only he were more like his sister, Gwen, two years older and much wiser. She didn't take crap from anyone. One night, a week after her sixteenth birthday, she vanished and never came back.

If Brady had his way, he would have stayed home, a mug of hot coffee at hand and his wife's just-baked apple crisp in front of him. But Robert had called, demanding one last hunt, so what choice did Brady have? Ever the peacekeeper. Brady sighed. His body felt damp and sticky despite the chill of late autumn. He inhaled, counted to four, then exhaled, apprehension about hunting with his dad creasing a line between his brows.

Robert opened his mouth to speak but seemed to think better of it. He had aged since Brady had last seen him. Yellowish pallor, thick veins roping his neck, lines looping around his lips and eyes. The ravages of a smoker.

Robert coughed into a soiled handkerchief, his head bobbing against his chest, and reached for a plastic flask tucked behind his seat. 'Oh, for Christ's sake,' he said when his efforts to remove the cap failed.

Brady took the flask and twisted off the lid. The smell of booze filled the air.

'Goddamned eyes,' Robert said. 'I used to have 20/20 eyesight. Did I ever tell you that? Better than 20/20 in fact. Doctors were amazed at how well I could see.'

'Yes, Pop. You've told me a hundred times.'

'Well, fuck you, then.'

'Let's not fight. Not today.'

'Up yours with a hose,' Robert said, chewing his bottom lip.

'Change of plans,' Brady said. 'Stay here and rest up a bit. I'll do the prep.' Brady pulled a buff-coloured cap over his slightly balding head before slinging a bag of decoys over his shoulder. 'Pop, maybe you can find your call-in show on the radio. I won't be long.'

Tracks from white-tailed deer dotted the route to the pond. The man-made habitat had served local waterfowlers well over the years. To the right of the pond stood a row of pines, an effective shield to approaching ducks. An abandoned silo jutted from the saw grass, serving as a perfect roost for silver-haired bats widespread in the district.

The rain had quit but would return soon judging by the indigo clouds bulging along the horizon. Holding up a spit-wetted finger, he tested wind direction; it was tailing in from the east. The dim light conditions were perfect. Brady could hardly wait for the sweet moment when day darkened to dusk, when ducks let down their guard and floated in to land. He plucked a handful of decoys from the canvas sack, donned his chest waders, and positioned the decoys into the water in a formation Robert had taught him when Brady was a boy. He would remain light on his feet, ready to reposition the decoys depending on the wind.

Brady removed his cap and scratched at his scalp through the sparse strands of hair left on top of his head. He couldn't recall exactly the last time they'd hunted together. Perhaps when Brady was ten or eleven, after his mother left. He still remembered her last words, spoken from where she stood with her back to the front door: *Enjoy yourselves.* His father's expression had been unreadable, the house eerily silent, and it stayed that way forever afterwards.

The blind jutted into the pond like a slice of pie. The decayed vegetation on the sides and roof offered a taupe canopy to ward off wary eyes while still giving the hunters full view of the sky. It was the ideal setup for a decisive finish. Brady headed back to meet his father. Within minutes his lungs were on fire. He was sorely out of shape. As Brady crested the last of the hills, Robert stepped from the truck, his Remington Model 870 Wingmaster dangling from his emaciated shoulder.

'The nap was just what the doctor ordered. I'm ready,' Robert said, his fingers tapping a victory dance against his chest. 'Let's do this.'

Father and son walked side-by-side for a time, their boots hitting the ground with unrehearsed synchrony. Robert's pants rustled with each step he took. The butt of his gun beat against his hip. But when the treads of Robert's boots filled with mud, he fell behind. Brady disappeared over a knoll. Robert's lips puckered to whistle but no sound came out. Tripping over the detritus littering the path, first one knee, then the other, gave way, causing him to crumble in a choreographed collapse of skin and bones.

Brady sensed his father was no longer keeping pace and ran back. 'Pop, you okay?' He bent down and seized his father's elbow.

'Let go of me. I'm fine,' Robert said, shaking Brady off.

Propping himself on Brady's leg, his lips parched and pale, Robert hoisted himself halfway. His grip on Brady's thigh was surprisingly fierce for a man in his condition. There was a brief wordless struggle. A blue tattoo peeked out of Robert's shirt from his chest. A radiation marker, a reminder to Brady of what his father had been enduring, alone, of how quickly the illness had progressed.

'Give me another second, damn it. I'll get there if it kills me.'

Once Robert was standing upright again, he trudged along slowly as if his boots were made of concrete. It didn't take long before he wobbled again, his bony bottom collapsing against his heels before he fell into the dirt.

Lying there, his fingers fumbled along the ridge of his ear, coming up empty. 'Where's my fucking cigarette?'

'You don't smoke anymore, remember?'

'The hell I don't.'

'The doctors said it would kill you if you didn't quit.'

'What the hell do they know? I'm dying anyway.'

Brady scooped his father up and half-carried, half-dragged him until he was completely winded and had to set his father down. 'You can tell the guys back at the old-age home that we tried.'

'Get my sorry ass to that blind.'

'Stubborn son-of-a—'

But there was no point in arguing with the old man. In a couple of hours it would all be over. Plump raindrops began to collect on the shoulders of Brady's coat. He didn't know if he should weep or whoop with joy. Steady precipitation pretty much guaranteed ducks would return to the pond for the night. By the weight and smell of the air, the rain would continue well into the evening. He hoisted his father onto his back.

'Let me down, damn it!' Robert's fists pounded Brady's back.

'We're almost there. Let me do this for you.'

With a sideways gait, Brady edged through rows of harvested corn toward the pond. Within twenty yards of the blind, Robert tumbled off his son's back.

'Look, near the point,' Robert said, squinting and pointing down the hill.

'It's just our decoys, Pop.'

The birds *did* look awfully real. The majority of decoys were commercial-grade machine-molded plastic. The larger decoys sported distinctive green heads of male mallards while the smaller ones had the dull colouring of females. A few were homemade, made from cork, primitive in shape and detail but highly effective at fooling ducks.

'I just hope I positioned the decoys right, like you or Uncle Al would have.'

'Don't be comparing yourself to experts. Anyway, you worry too much. Always have.' Robert turned his back. 'Time for a leak,' he said, fumbling with his trousers.

'Here, let me hold your gun.'

'It's the zipper. The damned thing is stuck.'

Robert's pants turned dark with urine. Brady averted his eyes. He should never have agreed to take his father on this hunt.

'That's it. Let's get you back for a change of clothes.'

'No way! We're here to hunt and we will do a hunt.'

Robert pushed past Brady and folded himself onto the bench

at the back of the blind. Measuring eight by ten, the frame consisted of two-by-twos driven into the ground. Brady had ensured that the blind melted into the landscape, just like Robert had taught him. Aspen branches and other dried debris concealed the entrance from apprehensive birds. The edges were stuffed with mud that now resembled honey gone hard. Brady sat beside his father, providing added support by pressing a thigh against Robert's bony hip.

Robert said, fierce pride etched on his face. 'They took my license.'

'Who?' Brady suspected that if his father were offered a choice between keeping his license and giving up sweat treats after lunch and supper, he'd have chosen his independence.

'The goddamned government, that's who. They say I can't be trusted now that the lung cancer is in my brain.'

'I heard.'

'Who told ya?' Robert asked.

'Doc Hansen. I was in last week about my prostate,' Brady said, slouching.

'See much of your sister?' Robert asked, bending to cough.

'Here and there. She's pretty preoccupied with work.'

A gust of wind whipped around the blind filling their nostrils with the thick, musty smell of the marsh.

Robert trained the metal barrel of his Wingmaster on a yet-to-be-determined target beyond the pond. As sick as he was, Brady thought, the old man still had it in him.

'See something?' Brady asked, releasing the lid on a container of soup. He offered his father a sip but Robert shook his head no.

'Not even the cook at the old-age home can coax me to eat these days.'

Robert coughed until he began to choke on the phlegm. Brady rubbed his father's back briefly before whispering, 'Pop, on your right.'

Five mallards were diving in from the west. Brady quietly screwed back the lid on the thermos, then lifted his Rich-N-Tone single reed call to his lips. His tongue control on the reed was accomplished and confident.

'Not as convincing as me, son, but pretty damn good.'

Brady could not remember the last time his father had paid him a compliment. He placed his arm loosely around his father's shoulder.

Robert trained his field glasses on a bird that had split unexpectedly from the flock. In the waning light, the duck cupped its wings and began its descent. The rush of the imminent kill was intoxicating.

'If you need help, say it.' Brady's voice was now less than a whisper.

Robert lifted the gun. His body stiffened with the weight of it, but he kept his eye trained on the bird all the while.

'I've got this,' Robert said, his blue eyes blazing.

Brady braced himself behind his father. He positioned the butt end of the gun against Robert's shoulder, held it steady, and murmured, 'Now.'

He felt the gun's action through his father's body, the recoil so powerful it tipped Brady onto his heels.

'Holy shit!' Robert said.

A second bird, a female, listed in from the other direction. 'Another one, Pop. Shoot.'

Robert pulled the trigger, the recoil again rippling through his body.

'Wow!' Brady whooped. 'I think you got her!'

Brady cinched the straps of his chest waders over his shoulders before stepping from the blind. He knew his father had missed both birds, but he spent fifteen minutes beating the reeds at the edge of the pond pretending to look for them. When he returned, he said he couldn't find either one.

'I know you winged them,' he said. 'But they must've flown off.'

'Jesus Christ!' Robert said. 'You idiot! Anybody else would've found them. Didn't you see which way they went?'

'I'm really sorry,' Brady said. He sat down on the bench and kept his shoulders hunched until Robert's anger wore itself out in a grinding, lung-rumbling cough. After that, the two men sat in silence for a long time. Then, in the gathering dark, Brady reached into the breast pocket of his shirt and pulled out the cigarette Robert had dropped on the trail.

'Here,' he said, with a threadbare smile. 'Maybe this'll make you feel better.'

TOOK YOU SO LONG

During the final assembly of the school year, I pumped my hand in the air, pleading with the firemen to select me for the 'stop, drop, roll' demonstration, but they chose Marty because he had the highest mark in gym. Grades one, two, and three were crammed together on the front lawn like worms in a can of bait. The grass was still soggy with morning dew. The fire truck was huge and as brilliant as Superman's cape. Once everyone scampered through the truck and blasted the siren, the principal dismissed us for early recess.

I ran up to my teacher. Mrs Stuart was older than my mother, her bottle-blonde hair sprinkled with traces of grey. It was worn in a sophisticated arrangement of tiny curls pressed close to her scalp. 'Mrs Stuart, my paper dolls are in the cloakroom. Can I get them?' My father had picked up the paper dolls for me after dropping my mother off at Princess Margaret Hospital. Two dolls made from cream-coloured cardstock—one boy and one girl. They each had four changes of clothes—one for every season. I had brought shorts, T-shirts and a blouse for them to change into.

Mom was in the hospital for some kind of procedure no one had yet explained to me. All I knew was that I wasn't allowed to visit while she was there.

Before she took sick, she used to pack my lunches with three hard-boiled eggs and a baggie of saltine crackers. She usually included grapes or an apple, and there were always a few home-made cookies, too. The school supplied complimentary white milk to anyone who wanted it. 'You need to grow,' my mother said, pinching the flesh of my upper arm.

During lunch I struck the eggs against the edge of the cafeteria table with great gusto before the shell released in pieces. That is, until Meg and Cora pointed out that my lunch smelled bad. 'Stinks to high heaven,' Meg liked to say. She wasn't the only one who hated me for my lunches. The other children had what everyone else had: sandwiches made from white bread sold in plastic sleeves at the grocery store, the pale, lightly baked dough spread with peanut butter and jam or soft cheese from a jar. They had cellophane packages of store-bought cookies.

Cora had a moon-face and flat nose. She wore black-rimmed glasses that needed constant thumbing to keep them in place. And she was a messy eater. Food stuck between her teeth and stains as red as blood speckled the front of her blouse. I was only in grade two, but I had already spent more than enough time wishing Cora and Meg would stop making me feel so worthless.

My desk was at the front of the row, by the windows and close to the chalkboard. Mrs Stuart kept a telephone book on my seat to help me see over my desk. Cora and Meg sat a couple of desks behind and a full row over.

Mrs Stuart let me go inside all on my own to get my paper dolls, as long as I promised to get them quickly and head straight out afterward. Once I had them and was back outside, I tucked myself into a corner near the custodian's entrance. It was the safest place to be when I had no one to play with. We were forbidden to hang out there, but I was so small I was practically invisible. I took a chance no one would notice.

Susan K. was my only friend, but she was at home recuperating from getting her tonsils out. She was the tallest person in our class and maybe the entire primary wing. When Susan was around, Meg and Cora didn't bother me with their shenanigans.

Anyway, Susan wasn't there and Meg and Cora soon tracked

me down. As they marched toward me, I pressed my back against the orange brick, willing the wall to swallow me up. My thighs pushed against the coarse tarmac, trying to keep the paper dolls and their outfits hidden. Despite the hot breeze, I shivered when Cora and Meg loomed over me, their shadows wide and sinister.

Meg was the fattest kid in the class. There were rolls around her belly. Her frizzy hair framed her face like tufts of milkweed, and she always smelled of talcum powder.

One time my mother asked why I'd come home with hair torn from my scalp. I didn't want to be rude by not answering but I didn't want to explain that no other girls in my class wore their hair the way she fixed mine. Cora made sure to remind me of my unfashionable hair. Violently.

Meg leaned over me and pointed at a paper doll poking from beneath my thigh. 'Them's for babies,' she said.

Cora said, 'Hand 'em over.' When I didn't immediately obey, her penny loafer kicked my leg. The shoe was dirty, and empty where the coin should have been. When I didn't budge, she kicked me again, harder. I tried to keep still but the pain caused my leg to lift. The dolls and their outfits fluttered away in a gust of warm wind.

'Ouch! What did you do that for?' I rubbed my thigh.

They laughed, a sound like squirrels chattering from a tree. Meg's lips pulled back to reveal a row of Chiclet-sized teeth. 'Let's go before the baby tells on us.'

'Hey,' was all I managed to say to their wobbling behinds. They'd gotten what they came for—they'd tormented me and left me quivering.

Once they'd gone, I scrambled after the lost dolls, my hands flailing uselessly overhead, trying to catch them. Too late. The dolls had already sailed over the fence that separated the farmer's field from the schoolyard.

I banged my fists against my forehead. 'Stupid, stupid,

stupid!' I said to myself. Then I headed for the door marked GIRLS. All of the stall doors were open so I knew I was alone. I was such a coward for letting them push me around. If Susan were here, she wouldn't let them get away with it. I pressed my face against the bathroom mirror, tears streaking down my cheeks.

* * *

Room 2 students were only allowed to use pencil, but that did not stop me from bringing a pen to class. It was no ordinary pen. It was a fountain pen. Not the kind with pre-filled plastic cartridges of blue or black ink, but the kind with a side lever for drawing into the chamber any colour you desired. I loved the weight of it in my hand, how the nib skated over the tooth of the paper. It was a cherished gift from my mother for getting all As in the first term.

My work always received gold stars, placed with care in the small space at the top of the page to the right of my name. Because I made it a habit to complete my work early, the teacher let me use pen to doodle in a scribbler. I was the only student in Room 2 permitted this privilege. Meg and Cora wanted a notebook like mine, another reason they hated me. They didn't earn gold stars, or any stars at all for that matter. Neither did Susan K., but that didn't prevent us from being friends.

Last period on Fridays was devoted to art. I loved art class. The other students looked happy, too, their tongues poking from the corner of their mouths like fish fillets. I used purple crayon to draw on cartridge paper. When the bell rang, I started to pull things out of my desk to pack up for dismissal. That's when I noticed that my pen wasn't where I'd left it. I took a gulp of air before hollering, 'Who took my pen?'

Snickers filled the air. Meg and Cora were smirking at me.

'They stole my pen!' I said, wiping my eye with a thumb.

'I'm glad. You shouldn't be allowed to bring a pen to school.' Meg said.

'Pack up, everyone.' Mrs Stuart pointed out the window to the river of mustard-coloured buses waiting to take us home.

Cora stuck out her tongue before heading for the cloakroom.

I didn't want anyone else to see me crying so I turned away. I sat at my desk, my eyes trained straight ahead while Mrs Stuart hurried everyone out.

'Oh, no,' she said. She flicked on the portable radio next to the chalkboard. Pop music spilled into the room. She opened her lunch sack and pulled out a candy bar.

'Here, have this. Then we'll see if we can't find that pen.'

I knew we'd never find it. I remained certain that either Cora or Meg had it. Instead of helping, I tore the wrapper off the candy bar and sank my teeth into a blend of nougat and peppermint.

After looking under desks, poking through crayon bins, and rifling through dirty socks and mittens in the lost and found bin, Mrs Stuart glanced at the clock and shrugged. 'I'm afraid I have to go pick up my daughter.' She crouched down so that she was at eye-level with me. 'Patsy, don't you worry. I promise we'll look for your pen first thing Monday.'

Shame intensified my despair. My parents would be so let down. I had lost something valuable. My mother would be terribly upset to learn how irresponsible I'd been. I still had no idea what was wrong with her, what had put her in the hospital. I worried this news would make her worse.

Mrs Stuart blew her bangs out of the way. 'Let's head down to the office and call your folks. They'll be mighty worried you're not home.' Why didn't Mrs Stuart remember that my mother wasn't home? But Mrs Stuart was in a hurry and left as soon as I opened the office door.

Back then, people living in the country shared a party line. By listening in, you got to know everyone's business.

The secretary dialed my number. 'Someone's on the line. I'll try again in a moment.'

I balanced on one foot, then the other while a large fan swivelled behind her. There was a bowl of paperclips next to her typewriter. I counted seventeen before she once again placed her hand on the handset. As she spun the rotary dial, clacking filled the space between us. 'We're having no luck, honey.' She glanced at the closed door to the principal's office.

My father was likely at the plant, or if he was home, he'd be with the chickens. I didn't tell her. I didn't want her raising her eyebrows any higher than she already had.

I puffed out my chest and looked her in the eye. 'My house isn't far,' I lied. 'Just over there.' I pointed out the office door. 'I've walked home plenty of times.'

The secretary glanced at the clock. 'I suppose if you've done it....' Before she changed her mind, I sprang for the foyer.

I skipped through the schoolyard, puffs of hot air lifting my skirt. Then I sat on a swing, closed my eyes, and made a plan. If I stuck to the road, I knew the way home like the back of my hand. It was a long walk, but I'd probably make it home for supper. On the other hand, if Susan K. were here, she'd say, 'Cut through the field. You'll shorten the trip by half.' I trusted Susan. Her family had horses and she rode them all over. She had probably taken the shortcut a million times.

Perched on the edge of the sandbox, I carefully considered the options. If I went home on the road, it would take way longer, which would make me late. My dad would worry. Besides, there were cars, and I risked getting hit. If I took the shortcut, I'd be home in half the time. As I climbed over the wire fence, I promised myself I would brag to my dad about how brave I was for finding my way home on my own.

On the other side of the fence, I checked for my paper dolls, but they were long gone. I looked further afield, a hand shading my eyes against the sun. From a nearby meadow, a cow's swim-goggle eyes gawked at me. I didn't know for sure if cows posed a danger, and I was pleased that she and the rest of the herd were in a different field than the one I would take to get home.

I maintained a decent speed for my first hundred steps along the fencerow. If I could keep that pace, I estimated I might be home in the time we get for gym class, about forty minutes. I found myself needing to take breaks, but whenever I stopped to catch my breath, the heat of the late afternoon sun became unbearable. The beating sun and the lack of water caused sweat to roll down my back. At least when I was walking, my body created a breeze. My underwear became damp with sweat, and I was soon overcome with weakness. I could hardly keep my eyes open. I somehow kept moving even though I was having a hard time walking straight.

My dad would be so angry if he came home to find the house empty. I could picture him sitting on the sofa in the living room, a hand-rolled cigarette between his lips, one hand on the telephone receiver while the other pawed through the directory for the school's number.

A tractor rumbled by in the next field over. I waved my arms but the farmer didn't slow down. 'Help!' I shouted, but my voice was drowned out by the sound of the engine. I slipped my backpack from my shoulder to see if there was anything left. After wolfing down the few remaining crumbs, I opened my thermos to find it dry.

I plucked clover and sucked sweetness from the tiny petals. By this time, I was beyond parched, but I knew I needed to take a rest. With no way to find good drinking water, I decided to lie down. I folded my backpack and used it as a pillow. Maybe if I rested for a while, I'd gain enough energy to get home. I lay there under the bright blue sky, my legs stuck together with sweat. Before long, my eyes closed.

I woke with a start to the sound of a light rain falling on the earth beside my head. My wrist burned where my other hand had held onto it. Overhead the sky was dark—not nighttime dark but the kind that comes when weather changes. I didn't mind. I opened my mouth to catch some raindrops. At least I could finally quench my thirst. The rain soothed my hot body. Refreshed I got up and started to run. My arms soon synchronized perfectly with my legs. My runners grew sticky as moist soil caked onto the soles. I ran until I felt like I couldn't breathe.

In the distance was a woodlot. I pushed through a patch of tall ferns, which led into an opening in the woods. I hoped it might be the same wooded area down the concession from my house. I eventually stumbled upon a narrow footpath through the woods. I followed it, and all the while, raindrops dribbled off the leaves and collected on my arms and head. I came upon a small parking lot. The lot was mostly sand and gravel, almost like a beach, only there was no pond or lake. There were lines in the sand made by tires. Cigarette butts and thin, rubbery balloons littered the ground. Water had collected in the depressions left by car tires.

I heaved a sigh of relief. 'I know where I am!' I yelled. Susan and I had been here one time when her dad had taken us horseback riding.

I ran until I reached the laneway to my house, a triumphant grin stretched across my face. I was no coward. I had conquered the unknown and faced adversity. I had pushed beyond the limits of my mind and body, and I'd done it with no one's help. I'd never felt so powerful in my life.

I pounded the screen door. 'Patsy,' my dad said before opening the door. I threw myself against his legs. I wondered if he could guess where I'd been all this time, what I'd done, how sneaky and clever I'd been. I could hardly wait for him to tell my mother what a brave girl I was.

My father's arms folded around my shoulders, efficient, strong, loving. He dropped to my level, his lips finding the part in my hair. 'What took you so long?' he said.

ACKNOWLEDGEMENTS

The stories in this collection were written at my home in Bruce County, which I acknowledge lies in the traditional territory of the Haudenosaunee (Iroquois), Ojibwe/Chippewa and Anishinaabeg, a territory covered by the Upper Canada Treaties.

Some of these stories have appeared in earlier forms in the following publications: *The Winnipeg Review*, *Fifteen Stories High*, *The Belle Journal*, *Rhubarb*, and *New Contrast*. Thank you to the editors who believed in my work.

Although all of these stories are works of fiction, their inspiration often came from life and asking 'what if'. I wish to acknowledge the influence of Cheryl-Ann Webster and her Beautiful Women Project installation in Southampton, Ontario on one of the stories.

Appreciation goes to Scott Walker, Director of CSARN, formerly known as Canadian Senior Artists' Resource Network, for recognizing the possibilities in my literary project. Thank you as well to my CSARN mentor, Max Layton, for your incredible support, gentle approach, and sage advice. You gave me the kicks I needed when I needed them, and you offered them with grace.

I would also like to thank my workshop pals at the Writers Roundtable in Paisley, and the gang of writers in Walkerton. You know who you are. Your early insights changed the stories for the better.

Heartfelt appreciation to Tim and Elke Inkster, owners of the Porcupine's Quill, for believing in this book and taking a chance on it. Thank you to Stephanie Small, editor, for your guidance. You helped me take the manuscript from its infancy to publication. Your attention to detail and excellent communication skills were appreciated. You were patient with me and always recognized when and how hard to push. I am forever indebted.

I am eternally grateful to my parents, who experienced many challenges as immigrants to Canada, but who agreed upon two things: their shared love for me, their only child, and the importance of education.

I also owe a world of thanks to my daughters, Carolyn and Kathleen, who acted as early readers of much of my writing. Through your patience and scrutiny, many of the early cracks in the manuscript were sealed. To my son, Cory, thank you for looking the other way when I elbowed you out of your bedroom at the cottage and turned it into my sacred writing space.

To my grandchildren, Kai, Mirabelle, and Zinnia: you are my muse. Remember, you can do anything you want if you put your mind and heart into it. Your Nana did!

Most of all, I owe this collection to my husband, John. Your love serves as my buoy. I'm indebted to your undying tolerance whenever I ruminated in my head instead of being in the present. These stories would not exist without your support.